"If I'm so good with the ladies, how come it hasn't worked on you?"

Her easy laughter filled the room. "I don't think you've been trying to charm me, only drive me away. Besides, I'm not a lady. I'm your physical therapist."

Ooh, she was definitely a lady. "Just out of curiosity, what would it take to get your… attention?" Dylan asked with a grin.

"More than sweet words…or a cocky smile. I have three brothers, and they've inherited a bit of the blarney along with their Irish genes." She sobered. "Besides, I learned a long time ago to believe only half of what men say."

"Who did you wrong? Want me to go beat him up?"

Sadness transformed her face. "You can't beat him up…he's dead."

Dear Reader,

Baby birds are chirping, bees are buzzing and the tulips are beginning to bud. Spring is here, so why not revive the winter-weary romantic in you by reading four brand-new love stories from Silhouette Romance this month.

What's an old soldier to do when a bunch of needy rug rats and a hapless beauty crash his retreat? Fall in love, of course! Follow the antics of this funny little troop in *Major Daddy* (#1710) by Cara Colter.

In *Dylan's Last Dare* (#1711), the latest title in Patricia Thayer's dynamite THE TEXAS BROTHERHOOD miniseries, a cranky cowboy locks horns with his feisty physical therapist and then learns she has a little secret she soon won't be able to hide!

Jordan Bishop wants to dwell in a castle and live happily ever after, but somehow things aren't going as she's planned, in *An Heiress on His Doorstep* (#1712) by Teresa Southwick. This is the final title in Southwick's delightful IF WISHES WERE…miniseries in which three friends have their dreams come true in unexpected ways.

When a bookworm meets her prince and discovers she's a real-life princess, will she be able to make her own happy ending? Find out in *The Secret Princess* (#1713) by Elizabeth Harbison.

Celebrate the new season, feel the love and join in the fun by experiencing each of these lively new love stories from Silhouette Romance!

Mavis C. Allen
Associate Senior Editor

Please address questions and book requests to:
Silhouette Reader Service
U.S.: 3010 Walden Ave., P.O. Box 1325, Buffalo, NY 14269
Canadian: P.O. Box 609, Fort Erie, Ont. L2A 5X3

Dylan's Last Dare

PATRICIA THAYER

THE
TEXAS
BROTHERHOOD

SILHOUETTE *Romance*®
Published by Silhouette Books
America's Publisher of Contemporary Romance

To Nora.
Thank you, niece, for your expertise in getting my hero back on his feet.
And to my model, Daniel. I couldn't have done it without you both.

Thanks to Colin Anderson for sharing your bull-riding experiences.
I know your wife and mom are happy you are retired.

And always to Hence, my friend and true Texas cowboy.

 SILHOUETTE BOOKS

ISBN 0-373-19711-X

DYLAN'S LAST DARE

Copyright © 2004 by Patricia Wright

Books by Patricia Thayer

PATRICIA THAYER

has been writing for sixteen years and has published nineteen books with Silhouette. Her books have been nominated for the National Readers' Choice Award, Virginia Romance Writers of America's Holt Medallion, Orange Rose Contest and a prestigious RITA® Award. In 1997, *Nothing Short of a Miracle* won the *Romantic Times* Reviewers' Choice Award for Best Special Edition.

Thanks to the understanding men in her life—her husband of thirty-two years, Steve, and her three grown sons and two grandsons—Pat has been able to fulfill her dream of writing romance. Another dream is to own a cabin in Colorado, where she can spend her days writing and her evenings with her favorite hero, Steve. She loves to hear from readers. You can write to her at P.O. Box 6251, Anaheim, CA 92816-0251, or check her Web site at www.patriciathayer.com for upcoming books.

All underlined places are fictitious.

Chapter One

Dylan Gentry's life would never be the same again.

He gripped the arms of his wheelchair, trying to fight off the panic that threatened to take over his already battered body.

It was all gone.

He'd never again be able to do what he loved. He'd never be able to feel the rush from a wild ride, the thrill from the cheer of the crowd as he broke out of the chute. He'd ended up a cripple for life, all because of one mean son-of-a-gun bull, Red Rock.

Dylan's hands fisted. He hated himself more for the self-pity. But dammit, hadn't he earned the right? He'd spent the last two months in the hospital. He'd had three surgeries, one to close up the wound in his gut from being hooked by the bull, and two more on his crushed leg.

Hell, it was January. He'd spent the entire month of December in the hospital. A month that he'd planned to spend at the national finals in Las Vegas. Now he was stuck in a two-bedroom cottage at his brother Wyatt's ranch in San Angelo, Texas, waiting for the next physical therapist to show his face.

In the past two weeks, he'd already sent six packing within hours after their arrival. Today, he was going for number seven. At least it gave him something to look forward to. He glanced around his new home. There was a state-of-the-art television and sound system, a bookcase filled with every top-selling novel.

There sure as hell wasn't much else for him to do.

He picked a book off the coffee table and threw it at the door, hating what he'd become and feeling sorry for the next person who walked in the door to face his wrath.

Brenna Farren stepped onto the small porch and raised her hand to knock on the door, when she heard something hit the other side. Startled, she paused, recalling what Wyatt Gentry had told her about his injured brother. No doubt the past months had been difficult for national-champion bull rider Dylan Gentry. As a physical therapist, Brenna knew she wasn't her patients' most popular person. She had known this was going to be a difficult job when she applied for the position, but she wasn't about to turn down the excellent pay and the bonus, which was she could live right here in the cottage.

Another object hit the door with a thud. Sounded as if her new patient was having a bad day. Even with her limited experience she knew that was to be expected.

Brenna gripped the knob. "Let's see if we can change that, Mr. Gentry," she said, then released a breath as she swung open the door. She walked inside and caught a surprised look from the good-looking man sitting in the wheelchair.

Midnight-black hair hung over his ears and forehead.

His square jaw showed more than a few days of scraggly beard, but that didn't take anything away from his handsome face. Yet it was his eyes that caused her to pause. They were a pale blue, mixed with silver. His gaze was cold as stone, yet triggered a sudden warmth within her.

She jerked away from his hold and smiled brightly at his irritated look. "Good morning, Mr. Gentry."

"Who the hell are you?" he growled.

"Brenna Farren."

"Well, if you're here to clean I don't need the sheets changed or any fresh towels."

She figured the towels didn't need to be changed, because he looked as if he hadn't bathed in days. She glanced around the mess in the cozy room. "The place could stand to be tidied up, but not right now. I'm here to help you get back on your feet. I'm your physical therapist."

He couldn't hide his surprise. "The hell you are."

"That's correct, I've been recommended by Dr. Morris, the orthopedic surgeon who took over your case when you moved here. Your brother hired me."

"Well, you can just tell Wyatt to unhire you because I don't need you."

"You need me more than you think, Mr. Gentry." Her gaze moved over him. Dressed as he was in a T-shirt, she could see his upper-body muscle tone was incredible. Her attention went to his cutoff sweatpants that allowed her to see the long scar running down his left calf. She tried to remain expressionless, but she knew that this man had had his share of pain, since his cast had been removed only three weeks ago. She also noticed that his inactivity from being in a wheelchair showed in his flaccid lower limbs.

"Not a pretty sight, is it?" he hissed.

He was a beautiful sight, just his leg was scarred. "I've seen worse," she admitted. "Besides, the scars will fade more as time passes."

"I don't give a damn."

"Well, I'm here to help change your mind about that."

"I don't need anyone," he snapped at her. "I'm doing just fine." He tried to move away, but the wheel caught on the end of the coffee table. Brenna watched as a frustrated Dylan fought to turn. Finally he broke free and rolled his chair across the room.

"First thing tomorrow I'll have some of this furniture removed to make it easier for you to move around," she called to him.

Dylan Gentry stopped at the wide bedroom door. "Don't waste your time, Ms. Farren. You won't be here tomorrow." His large hands worked with the wheels and he rolled himself inside the room and slammed the door.

Brenna released a long breath. "That went well."

She walked though the living area. There was another door that led to the second bedroom. That was to be hers. She peeked inside. Although small, there was plenty of room for the double bed with a multicolored quilt and a tall pine dresser. The bathroom was roomy, and the doorway had been widened to accommodate a wheelchair. On the side of the tub was an attached whirlpool. Great.

She returned to the living room, then to the small dining area. At the table there was an empty spot for a wheelchair. Everything had been newly renovated to accommodate a handicapped person. Past the breakfast bar, she went to the refrigerator and opened the door, finding it fully stocked with food. More than likely Maura Gentry had brought meals in for her brother-in-law, but by the looks of it, he hadn't been eating much. She would have to change that since Dylan couldn't keep up any kind of strenuous exercise without some nutrition.

If he would cooperate with her. That meant somehow she had to get him to agree to do therapy. Her job depended on it. Even though her family was close by, she needed this job…and a place to live. As a recent graduate and with her present…circumstances, she didn't have the time to wait around for other offers.

Her mentor, Dr. Morris, had sent her to the Rocking R Ranch to talk with Wyatt Gentry about his twin brother who'd been seriously hurt during a bull-riding accident. Even after hearing that Dylan Gentry had driven off a half-dozen therapists in the past weeks, she hadn't been scared off. She couldn't afford to be.

Still, she knew this had to be rough on the two-time world-champion bull rider. She should add the best-looking man she'd ever seen. Those grainy black-and-white pictures in the paper hadn't done him justice. No doubt his reputation with the ladies wasn't an exaggeration. Now he was confined to a wheelchair.

It was Brenna's job to help change that.

Even when Wyatt had been reluctant to hire a woman, she had convinced him that she could handle the man and his therapy, promising she could get his brother back on his feet.

And Wyatt was giving her two weeks to get Dylan started on his exercise program.

Brenna was a West Texas native, had grown up on a ranch with brothers who'd ridden in a few rodeos. She could never figure out what drove some men to danger. The thrill of an eight-second ride, a ride that could be the last. Memories of Jason came rushing back as she recalled his fatal hang-gliding accident, and their argument that had been the last words spoken between them. Tears flooded her eyes, knowing he'd chosen the thrill of danger over her…and their unborn child. Now she was alone, pregnant and trying to survive the best she could.

Several loud thuds from somewhere in the cottage had Dylan burying his head under the pillow. He hadn't slept much last night, not when a picture of Brenna Farren appeared every time he closed his eyes. Hell, what did he expect? He hadn't been with a woman in months. So the first good-looking one to come along was bound to arouse him. The noise grew louder. He raised his head and glanced at the clock: 7:00 a.m. What was going on?

He grabbed a pair of sweats off the floor and dragged them on. Scooting to the edge of the bed, and with one arm on his wheelchair and bracing his weight on his good leg, he made it into the seat. He lifted his damaged leg onto the footrest, released the chair's brake, then headed to find the ruckus. He opened the door to discover that the red-haired vixen had returned.

Kneeling in the corner, Brenna Farren was attempting to pull out some shelves. The business suit she had on yesterday had been replaced with a pair of faded jeans that hugged her shapely bottom and two long…lovely legs. A pale pink blouse didn't hide her other generous curves, either. Her long hair was pulled back into a ponytail, showing off a slender neck and creamy skin. He shook off a sharp tingling that suddenly added a different kind of pain to his lower body. Dammit, she wasn't supposed to be back.

"I told you yesterday I didn't need your services, Ms. Farren."

She swung around, the look of surprise widening her

huge whiskey-brown eyes. "Oh, good morning, Mr. Gentry."

"There's nothing good at this hour."

"Oh, really." She sat down on the floor. "I love the early morning. It's so quiet…peaceful." Her voice was soft and throaty, reminding him of dim morning light and whispered demands of lovers… He shook off the thought.

"That's because everyone is asleep," he argued. "That's what I want to be."

"You can sleep in later after we get you on a routine."

"When hell freezes over," he said and nodded toward the door. "Now, would you mind leaving?"

She stood up and placed her hands on her hips. "As a matter of fact, I would mind. I promised your brother that I'd give this job a chance—that I wouldn't let your rude attitude run me off. So you'll have to do better than shout at me. I grew up with three brothers. I've been yelled at by the best."

Dylan's fists clenched. He loved Wyatt but he was getting pretty tired of his interference. "Then I'll pay you for the month and fire you."

She shook her head. "You can't do that. I took this job and I made a promise. Now, you've already spent too much time in that chair without working your muscles. It's going to be even harder to get you up and walking—but not impossible."

"You don't seem to understand, Ms. Farren."

"Brenna," she corrected.

He sighed. "Brenna. I can't get back on my feet. I'm going to be in this chair for the rest of my life."

Brenna could see the fear in his eyes and heard it in his voice. She had a strange impulse to reach out and touch him, to give him comfort. She pulled back. "How do you know that, Dylan? I've conferred with your physician, and he said you haven't given therapy enough of a chance."

"You discussed my case?"

"With Dr. Morris," she said bravely. "We've gone over your X rays and I talked with Dr. Ratner, the surgeon in California who did the reconstruction. He did a remarkable job."

"Then why the hell aren't I walking?"

"Because the damage was severe. Besides a rod put in to repair your tibia, pins were added to the talus bone."

"Speak English."

"All right. Your left calf and ankle were crushed by a two-thousand-pound bull. Not only the bones, but there was some muscle and nerve damage. It's important you do therapy to help with circulation and to strengthen the muscles. I also know the bull's horn punctured your abdomen and you sustained rib damage, but you healed nicely. So that pain shouldn't stop you."

"Well, I'm stopping you," he argued. "I've heard it all before by several specialists. Bottom line is they couldn't guarantee that I could go back to riding, or even that I'll walk again. Okay, okay, I should consider myself lucky to be alive. But lady, I don't call this living. And I'm not going to bust my butt for nothing—not if I can't be like before." He turned his chair around and returned to his bedroom.

Brenna wanted to call him back, but Dylan clearly wasn't ready to hear anything she had to say. Not now. It was her job to get him to want to give therapy a chance. How was she going to challenge this man?

Somehow she had to make him want to fight to walk again.

There was a quiet knock on the door and Wyatt Gentry peeked his head in. He smiled and, although the two men weren't identical twins, she could see the close resemblance.

Wyatt walked in. "Should I ask how things are going?"

"Not bad," she lied. "Your brother hasn't thrown anything at me."

"Give him time." Wyatt grew serious. "Brenna, if you've changed your mind and think this job is too much, I'll understand."

Oh no, she couldn't lose it before she got a chance. She shook her head. "Trust me, I can handle anything that Dylan dishes out. I just have to figure out a way to make him want to try therapy."

"Well, I hope you make it. Oh, by the way, the parallel bars are being delivered within the hour. Just tell me what you want removed from the room."

"We can do without the bookshelves, the recliner chair and coffee table. If it's not too much trouble. That will give us room for the weight bench and bars."

"This is the easy part," he assured her. "Dealing with Dylan's temper is the difficult task. Maybe I should be here when he sees what's going on."

"No. That's why you hired me. I have to be the one he communicates with. Your brother is used to getting what he wants. He has to learn that if he wants to walk again, he has to work at it."

Wyatt grinned. "I'm beginning to believe you can do it. It's been a long time since Dylan hasn't been able to sweet-talk a woman into getting his way."

Brenna tensed. The man was hard to resist, but not

for her. Right. She knew if Dylan Gentry wanted to, he could make her forget her own name. She just had to keep that fact from him. "You don't have to worry about me being charmed by your brother. I'm his therapist...that's all." It would be a long time before she would allow herself to be interested in any man, much less a danger-loving man like Dylan Gentry.

By 11:00 a.m. the furniture had been removed and the parallel bars and weight bench had been set up in the living area, leaving just enough space for the TV and sofa. Brenna decided that her patient wasn't going to have enough energy left after therapy to do anything else but watch TV.

Speaking of her patient, she hadn't seen Dylan since earlier in the morning. Well, it was time he came out of hiding. She went to his bedroom door and knocked.

There was only silence and she knocked again. "Dylan," she called.

No answer.

"Dylan? I'm fixing some lunch. Is there anything special you want?" Her job description also included making meals and some light housework. She didn't mind, since she was living here, too.

No answer.

"Dylan?" She knew he had to be hungry, because he hadn't had breakfast. "Are you all right?" She turned the knob and pushed open the door to find a large bed with Dylan Gentry sprawled across the center. A colorful quilt covered part of his body, but his glorious chest was bare. No red-blooded woman would deny that the man was beautifully built.

Surprised at the sudden rush of feelings, she refocused her thoughts and moved to the bed. He was her patient.

That was all. She called his name again. When that didn't wake him, she touched his foot. "Dylan, you need to get up."

The man opened his eyes, revealing mesmerizing silver-blue pools that immediately locked on her. A hint of a smile creased his sensual mouth.

"Well, hello, darlin'." He stretched his arms over his head, lazily. "I was just having this great dream, but you're so much better."

The husky tone of his voice sent a warm shiver though Brenna as she saw the true side of the charming bull rider that all the ladies drooled over. Well, she didn't have the time or the desire.

Brenna pushed away from the doorjamb and moved to the bed. "Well, you're not dreaming now," she said. "It's reality time."

His smile only grew as he rolled to his side and reached out to touch her arm. "The real thing is so much better." His voice turned husky. "Why don't you climb into bed and let me show you."

If his sexual advances were supposed to scare her off, he was wrong. She had heard similar words so many times before. Jason used to sweet-talk her every time he wanted his way. "I have a better idea. Why don't you get up and eat something, then do a short therapy session."

"The only place I'm headed is the bathroom, then back to bed." He sat up and the covers dropped to his waist as he reached for the wheelchair. Brenna was quicker and pulled it back, away from his reach.

"What the—?" His dark eyebrows drew together as he frowned at her. "What do you think you're doing?"

"You've been spending far too much time in this

chair. You need to get ambulatory. You're weakening your good leg by not using it."

"So what if I am?" he said. "That's my business."

"And *you're* my business."

"You're fired. Now get out."

She folded her arms. "Make me," she challenged.

Pain flashed across Dylan's face and Brenna wondered if she'd gone too far. She went into the living room, grabbed the walker and returned to the bedroom. "Here. From now on you'll use this to get around."

"You've got to be kidding," he said, disgust in his tone.

"If you can balance on the back of a bull, Mr. Dylan 'The Devil' Gentry, surely you can manage a walker."

He dropped backward on the bed. "I'm not using any damn walker...I'll crawl first, so you might as well give me back the chair."

"Physical therapists are a stubborn bunch. And since you're the one who has to use the bathroom, I think I can wait you out."

He pulled the quilt over his head and let out a string of colorful curses.

Brenna knew if she was going to work with Dylan, she couldn't let him get away with sleeping all day. She also knew that if he complained enough, Wyatt would fire her.

"You're behaving childishly, Mr. Gentry," she said as she took hold of the edge of the covers and yanked them away. She bit back a gasp, discovering the man was naked underneath. Quickly she diverted her eyes to his face, only to catch a satisfied grin from Dylan.

The man had absolutely no problem with his nudity. "Since we're getting so familiar with each other, don't you think you could call me Dylan? *Bren.*"

She dropped the blanket on him. "I'll call you whatever you like as long as you get up and attempt to cooperate."

He looked thoughtful. "All right, I'll get up, but only if I can use crutches."

"But your balance…"

Another grin. "Lady, like you said, my livelihood was dependent on my balance. Besides, I've used crutches a few times over the years with other minor injuries. So if you want me up, just bring me the damn things."

She left the room and by the time she returned with lightweight crutches, he'd managed to put on a pair of sweatpants. "This is against my better judgment," she told him. "You could fall."

"Darlin', I've been falling all my life," he said as he scooted to the edge of the bed.

"Not on my watch," she argued, then braced herself in front of him, planted her legs and helped pull him onto his good leg. Surprisingly, he did the task easier than she had expected. She helped him with the placement of the crutches, and walked along with him to the bathroom. She started to go in with him, but he stopped her.

"Whoa, this is where I draw the line. Sometimes a man has to go it alone. This is one of those times."

"What if you fall?"

"Then I pick myself up." He took another step inside and closed the door in her face.

"Just call out when you're finished, I'll come get you," she said through the door.

"I'm sure I can figure it out," she heard him say.

"You just think you can, Mr. Dylan 'The Devil' Gentry." She pivoted and marched to the kitchen, praying that she could survive this next month…and this man.

* * *

Dylan cursed as he stumbled coming out of the bathroom. Although he wasn't very good at it, he liked to be up, at least on his *one* good leg, but he wasn't going to let Ms. Farren know that.

With the crutches securely in place under his arms, he slowly made his way to the kitchen, still peeved he hadn't scared her off with his seduction routine. He found her at the stove, humming a song. Well, she wouldn't be singing for long, not after he tossed her out.

"As soon as you finish here, you better go pack your bags because you're not staying."

She turned and came to his aid. "Let's get you to the table, Dylan. The soup is nearly ready."

It did smell good, and he discovered he was hungry. He thought about telling her he didn't need any help, then her hands were on him. Although her gesture was clinical, he liked her gentle and warm touch. He also liked her nice scent, fresh…feminine. At the table, she was careful of his injured leg, and helped him into the chair. Then she came back with two bowls and placed one in front of him and took the seat across from him.

Brenna placed a napkin on her lap and looked up. Dylan couldn't help but notice how pretty she was. Not in a traditional beauty-queen fashion, but with startling warm, honey-brown eyes that seemed to hold such wonder and innocence, and her mouth had him wondering how it would taste. Her skin was flawless, despite a soft sprinkling of freckles across her pert nose.

No, he couldn't have her around. He didn't need anyone seeing him like this, especially a woman. "Look… you've got to face it, this isn't going to work. I don't want you here. So why don't you just leave?"

"I can't." She placed her spoon on the table. "To be honest, I need this job. But more important, Dylan, you need me. If you ever want to walk again, you need my determination, my drive to push you hard. You need someone who won't let you bully them. Who won't let you slack off. Oh, you need me all right—that is, if you ever want to regain the use of your leg.''

Her optimism was contagious, but he couldn't let himself hope. ''But I'll never climb back on a bull again.''

She huffed out a breath. ''Aren't two national championships enough? Besides, aren't you a little over the hill for a bull rider?''

Even though her comment was true, it still stung. Over thirty, everyone knew a rodeo rider was pretty much used up. He'd planned that this would be his last year. Of course, if he'd won the championship again, he probably would have gone another year on the circuit. ''I was on top this year. I was headed to the national finals in Las Vegas.'' He paused, realizing his frustration. ''How would you feel if you couldn't do your job?''

''It would be rough. But I'm trying to build my career, you've had years of success. Isn't being on top a good time to get out? Look at Michael Jordan, he retired.''

''Then he returned to basketball.''

She thought again. ''How about football players John Elway and Troy Aikman? They retired because of injuries that threatened their lives,'' she added. ''They found other things that were important to them. Surely you've made enough money to start over with something else. Besides, Dylan, you can't even walk right now. How can you think about going back?''

''That's what I mean,'' he stressed. ''So, what's the use of me killing myself if it's all for nothing?''

Brenna's eyes flashed as she got up from the table. ''The use is that you have other things to walk for. Your family. Your brother, his wife and their children.''

Dylan was never one to do much with family. Wyatt had been the only relative he had had, until last year when they'd learned their father's true identity. A bronc rider named Jack Randell. After the discovery, Wyatt immediately had to come to San Angelo, Texas, even bought the old Randell family ranch, the Rocking R. Dylan had wanted no part of the Randells, but Wyatt had gotten close to his half brothers, Chance, Cade and Travis, and their other illegitimate half brother, Jared Trager.

And since the accident, Dylan had been stuck here. "That's Wyatt's family, not mine."

"It's yours, too," she insisted. "Family can be important to your rehabilitation."

He didn't want to hear any more. "What is it going to cost me to get rid of you?"

Brenna crossed her arms over her breasts. Just the simple movement was erotic. Oh, God. He couldn't have her living here.

"Why don't I make a deal with you," she began. "How about you cooperate with me for two weeks?" She raised her hand to stop him. "Just hear me out."

He hesitated, then gave a nod.

"If there isn't any progress by that time, I'll leave." She lowered her hand. "Now, I have terms. I want you to get out of bed every morning by seven o'clock, you'll need to spend the allotted time on the parallel bars and work twice a day with weights. And I will work you hard, Dylan. Harder than you've probably had to work in your life, but I also believe that together we can get results." She looked him in the eye. "You can walk, Dylan. I believe it. So, how much are you willing to do for that? How much are you willing to do so you can get out of the wheelchair, to walk on your own?"

Dylan didn't want to just walk, he wanted to go back to what he had loved to do: bull riding. He wasn't afraid of work. Hell, he grew up with hard manual labor, handling rough stock for rodeos. But this was all he'd ever wanted. And even if he was retiring, he wanted to go out on top. He was Dylan "The Devil" Gentry.

"I want to get back to rodeoing. Can you help me do that?"

He watched her hesitate and his heart sank into his gut. Then her eyes darkened with determination. "It's going to cost you extra, but I feel if the desire is there, you can do anything."

"I know I have the desire, but do you, Brenna? Can you put up with my nasty attitude and bad days, and make me the man I used to be?"

"I hope by the time I'm finished you'll learn that being a man has nothing to do with the size of the bull you ride."

She made him want to do a lot more than just walk. He shook away the distracting thought. "Can you do it?" he challenged. "Will you do it?"

Brenna's gaze locked with his. There was a flicker of vulnerability before she masked it and nodded. "Why do I feel like I just sold my soul to the devil?"

His face split into a beautiful smile that set her heart aflutter.

Because she had.

Chapter Two

Early the next morning Brenna stepped outside on the porch, hoping the brisk air would help her recent queasiness. What she didn't expect was to find Wyatt Gentry's four-year-old daughter, Kelly, sitting on the step.

"Well, good morning."

Smiling, the cute little blonde stood. "Hi, Miss Brenna." Under a heavy nylon jacket, she wore a pink sweater with blue corduroy pants and a pair of boots. She came up another step. "You remember me? Kelly. I live in that house." She pointed to the large ranch house about a hundred yards away.

"Yes, Kelly, I remember you." Brenna hugged her own heavy sweater closer to ward off the January cold. "What are you doing out so early?"

"I'm going for a ride on my pony, Sandy. My daddy is going to take me." She frowned. "But I don't know where he is." She glanced at the cottage door. "Is he inside with Unca Dylan?"

"No, but your uncle is awake. You want to come inside?"

The girl shook her head, a mixture of fear and sadness in her eyes. "No. He doesn't like me."

"Oh, sweetheart. Your uncle was hurt in a bad accident. He's just having a rough time trying to make his leg work again. I bet soon he'll be happy again."

"Then will he like me?"

"I think he already does," Brenna tried to assure her. "But let's give him a few weeks and when he's feeling better you can come by for a visit."

The child smiled. "I like you," she said as she studied Brenna. "You're pretty. Do you have any little girls who are four?" She held up the same number of fingers.

Brenna shook her head as she held a protective hand over her stomach. "No, I don't," she said, feeling a sudden yearning. "Not yet." She prayed that the baby growing inside her would be born healthy. If she survived the next few months, this job paid well enough to guarantee that she could stay home with her child for those first few months, but she still couldn't give her baby a father.

A man's voice drew their attention and they both looked toward the barn to find Wyatt. Kelly's face lit up and she took off running. Brenna waved and watched until the girl jumped into her father's arms. The scene reminded her of her own father, Sean Farren. There was nothing like the secure feeling parents gave a child. Brenna was a little ashamed she hadn't told her parents about the baby—the baby she had conceived out of wedlock—with a man they'd never met.

Brenna knew they'd be disappointed with their oldest child and their only daughter. She was the first Farren to bring home a college degree. She also thought she'd be bringing a husband, but that had changed with Jason's hang-gliding accident and death. Just days later she'd discovered she was pregnant. With no other options, she had to come home to her family's ranch.

That was the reason she needed to have a job that paid enough to allow her to raise her child and not have to depend on Mom and Dad. Tugging her sweater around her, she knew she had to tell them. She'd seen the subtle changes in her body. At three months, she was beginning to lose her waistline. It wouldn't be much time before her secret was out.

Brenna walked back inside the cottage. This was to be her home for a while. But what would happen with her job when Dylan Gentry discovered her condition? Would he send her packing or would she be given the chance to help him back on his feet?

She hoped the latter. At least she didn't have to worry about the man being attracted to her. Most men ran from women with children. Too bad she couldn't say the same. The handsome bull rider was dangerous in more ways than one. She would definitely have to keep her head, and her distance.

Brenna glanced around the small but comfortable room. The cottage had been recently remodeled by Wyatt and Jared Trager. There were new windows, kitchen cabinets and countertops. The doorways had been widened and new hardwood floors had been laid throughout, making it easy to get through with a wheelchair.

Suddenly Dylan's bedroom door swung open and he came out with the aid of his crutches. She stayed rooted to the spot, waiting to see if he needed her assistance. By the looks of his sure, smooth movements, he was handling them very well. She figured he did everything well. There was one problem she thought, eyeing his perfectly proportioned body, his broad shoulders and bare chest. How could she get him to wear more clothes? Pregnant or not, her hormones were racing full speed, especially with a good-looking man around all the time.

"What's for breakfast?" he asked.

"So you're hungry?"

He made his way to the table. "If we're going to work this morning, I'm going to need some food. I've done enough weight training to know that."

A thrill rushed through Brenna. Her job had just become a whole lot easier. She walked into the kitchen and took the lid off the skillet that held the scrambled eggs and bacon she had prepared a short while ago. Taking out two plates, she scooped up the food and took them to the table. She went back for two glasses of juice. During the meal the conversation was kept at a minimum as her patient concentrated on his food.

Dylan paused from his eating and glanced across the table at his new drill sergeant, for the moment. Brenna looked a little tired and there were dark circles around those striking brown eyes. Of course, he was probably the reason. He hadn't exactly been agreeable since her arrival. He still didn't want her here and had planned to get rid of her, but she'd managed to find his weak spot.

She'd challenged him. And he'd never backed down from a challenge.

Besides, she was the only therapist who'd showed up at the door who seemed sure he would walk again. He still wasn't certain that she could pull it off. Although she wasn't very big in size, he knew she was strong. He'd felt the toned muscles across her back and arms when she'd helped him stand at the parallel bars yesterday.

Of course, she had to be strong to lift patients. What had surprised him was her embarrassment when she'd stripped off the blanket and discovered him buck naked. Hadn't she seen patients naked before? Hadn't she seen a man without clothes? He couldn't help but wonder if there was someone in her life.

She definitely was attractive enough. Although he preferred blondes, he wondered how that glorious rust-colored mane would look down. She smelled good, too. He remembered the soft citrus scent whenever she'd gotten close to him.

His attention turned to her figure. Although she was wearing bulky sweats now, he recalled the sweet curve of her hips and long slender legs. He had no doubt she would fill out a pair of Wranglers to perfection. Just the way he liked...

Whoa. He didn't need to think of Ms. Farren as anything short of Attila the Hun. He was already too vulnerable with his battered and bruised body. There were scars that would never go away. His leg was the worst, a road map of red lines from the accident and the numerous surgeries. Not a pretty sight.

There was a time when women had admired his physique. After every successful ride, he could almost guarantee there would be women who'd be willing to share his celebration, even the night, with him. Since the accident, they hadn't been exactly lined up at his door. Yesterday morning, for a flash of an instant, Brenna had looked at him as if he were a man. And he definitely saw her as a woman.

Man, she was going to be a killer on his sleeping schedule.

He downed his orange juice, then reached for his coffee mug and leaned back in his chair while watching her. She picked at her food. "At the rate you eat, I'll never get to the bars."

She set down her fork. "I guess I put too much on my plate." She stood. "You're right, we should get started." She carried the dishes to the sink.

"Hey, we have time for you to finish."

"I've had enough," she told him. "Drink your coffee and we'll get started on the weights."

"Why don't you join me with a cup?"

She shook her head. "Caffeine makes me jittery. But enjoy yours while I clean up the dishes."

"Can't we take a few minutes to talk?"

Brenna set the dishes on the counter and turned around. She knew it wasn't unusual for a patient and PT to get personal. "What would you like to know? My credentials?"

He shrugged. "Where are you from?"

"I grew up here. My parents own a small ranch on the other side of San Angelo."

"Does everyone around here ranch?" he asked.

She shrugged. "It *is* cattle country." She knew he was new to the area. "Your own family has done very well in the business." Everyone knew the affluence of the Randells.

"What family is that?"

"The Randells."

"Does everyone know my business?"

Brenna wiped her hands on a towel and came to the table. "No, I only know the story because Wyatt told me. If you're worried about what people think…"

"I don't give a damn, but my business is my business."

"Seems to me you gave up your privacy when you become a national bull-riding champion." She had seen

Dylan Gentry's exploits written up in the news the past years. "You draw a crowd wherever you go…especially women."

She saw a flash of pain in Dylan's eyes before he masked it. "That's over," he said. "I just want to be left alone."

Good. Brenna didn't feel like fighting off a bunch of women to get him to do his therapy. "That's fine with me." She pointed to the equipment in the living room. "We're going to be concentrating so hard on your rehab that you aren't going to have a chance to think about anything else."

He made a snorting sound. "There isn't enough therapy in the world to do that."

Brenna knew that dealing with a patient's depression was part of the job. Silently she went back to doing the dishes, knowing that she had to keep Dylan Gentry distracted with hard work.

Thirty minutes later, after a series of warm-up exercises, they got busy at the weight bench. Brenna was spotting Dylan as he lay on his back lifting the barbells up and down to help improve his upper-body strength. She was impressed at how easily he did each repetition. She also saw the strain on his face and knew he was pushing himself—too hard. Maybe he was just trying to impress the new PT, but she didn't want him to burn out. Finally she called a halt and handed him a towel to wipe off his sweaty chest. After a few minutes, she crouched in front of him and began strapping small weights around his ankles.

"We'll take this slow…and easy." She held on to his leg before he started. "We're not going all out on your first time, or tomorrow you'll be worthless. So take it easy," she warned. "Just lift your leg a few inches, hold it, then lower it."

A cinch, Dylan thought. But the light weight felt like a ton. By the time he finished five reps, beads of sweat had formed on his face. Even though she told him that was enough, he did five more. He wouldn't give her the satisfaction of seeing how hard the exercise was on him, but his leg had other ideas. The muscles fatigued from being sedentary for so long suddenly went into spasm.

Crying out, Dylan grabbed his leg. "Damn, damn…"

"Lie back," Brenna ordered as her sure hands went to work, kneading and soothing the knotted muscles in his thigh.

Dylan draped his arm over his eyes, hating his weakness but letting her magic fingers take over and ease his pain. Soon the pain turned to pleasure. What had soothed him was now beginning to arouse.

"That's enough." He sat up and tried to push her hand away. "My leg feels better."

"Just let me finish working out the stiffness."

He groaned and tightened his hold on her hand. "That's never going to happen if you keep this up," he said honestly.

She glanced down and suddenly her face flamed red. "Oh… Then we should take a break." She handed him a bottle of water and walked out of the room.

Dylan fell back on the weight bench and closed his eyes. Somehow, he had to find a way to stop seeing Brenna Farren as a woman. He thought about the long-legged, auburn-haired vixen and realized that was never going to happen.

Four days later, taking a break from his workouts, Dylan sat on the sofa, remote in his hand, flipping through the channels, when his brother peered in the door. "Hey, Dylan," Wyatt said. "Got a minute?"

"It's your house."

His brother frowned. "I told you when I bought the ranch months ago I want you as my partner, just like we'd always talked about."

"Didn't plan on me being a cripple."

"Temporary situation," Wyatt said assuredly.

"And I told you I want no part of the Randell place. Besides, if I had a choice…"

Wyatt raised his hand. "You wouldn't be here," he finished his brother's sentence. Wyatt sat down on the sofa. "Just so you know, this ranch didn't start with Jack Randell. Our grandfather, John Sr., started the Rocking R and was well respected in the community. At one time this spread was one of the biggest in the area until Jack ran it into the ground."

"And you're putting it back together." At his brother's nod, Dylan went on, "And you're even running a herd."

Wyatt nodded again. "Hank Barrett suggested I give it a try. The Rocking R's herd is for the Mustang Valley Guest Ranch's cattle drives and roundups." He folded his arms. "You can't believe the big demand for working cattle ranches."

Dylan saw his brother's excitement and envied him.

"Chance, Cade and Travis will be helping out," Wyatt continued. "I'd like you to meet them."

"Thanks, I think I'll pass."

Dylan had heard more than enough about his three half brothers and Hank Barrett, the man who raised them when Jack Randell was sent off to prison for cattle rustling. Dylan felt the same about Jared Trager, another illegitimate brother who'd showed up last year. Seemed their daddy enjoyed seducing women, then when he got tired of them, he moved on. And no one had seen anything of good old Jack for years.

"Maybe when you get back on your feet you'll feel differently," Wyatt suggested. "How is the therapy coming?"

Dylan frowned. "You should know since Ms. Farren has been reporting to you."

"Brenna and I haven't spoken since the day I hired her. I thought you should handle this business on your own."

Dylan gave a sarcastic hoot. "That would be a first." His brother had always tried to manage his life.

"Look, Dylan. A few months ago, I wasn't sure you would even survive the accident, let alone ever walk again," he said, emotion lacing his voice. "You've been given a second chance, but it's up to you what you do with it." Wyatt gave him a long look, then stood and walked to the door. "Call if you need anything." He left, closing the door quietly behind him.

Dylan suddenly felt like a heel. Deep down, he knew his brother was only trying to help him.

"Wyatt!" he called as he struggled to get up, one hand gripping the back of the chair as he reached for his crutches. He made it to the door, but when he pulled it open he was surprised when he was forced backward as someone slammed into him. It wasn't Wyatt, but Brenna. He fought to regain his balance but the attempt was futile. He dropped his crutches, reached out to grab the door frame for support, and in the process managed to sandwich Brenna between himself and the wall.

She gasped and her arms immediately went around his waist. He tried to shift his weight, but the action only seemed to increase the friction between them, shooting heat throughout his body.

"Dammit. Hold still," he demanded.

She froze. Only the sound of the TV in the background and their ragged breathing filled the room. Then her gaze raised to meet his and the startling color of her whiskey eyes mesmerized him. He couldn't seem to manage his next breath, but he managed to inhale her arousing scent. Only inches from her tempting mouth, he could easily bend forward and take a taste of her. Suddenly realizing where his thoughts were heading, he gripped the door frame and hopped backward on his good leg.

Now free, Brenna moved swiftly to retrieve his crutches. She helped slip them under his arms but didn't move away.

"You okay?" she asked.

He managed a nod, wishing she would stop asking him that question.

"Here, let me help you." Her hands touched his arms.

He jerked away. "I can do it," he insisted, and planted the base of his crutches on the floor, then turned and headed to the privacy of his bedroom. There he could deal with a different kind of pain.

Dylan didn't come out of the bedroom for the next hour. He didn't want to, at least not until he could find a way to fight his reaction to this woman. She was his therapist, she was going to have her hands on him…a lot. He groaned, thinking how much he wanted her touch…how he ached for it.

What the hell was wrong with him? No doubt Brenna was pretty, but she had commitment written all over her. And he definitely wasn't a forever kind of guy. Maybe in that respect he was like his old man. He had no desire to settle down with a wife and kids. He'd never known anyone who'd set a good example for him to follow.

All his life he and Wyatt had been known as Sally Gentry's bastard kids. Still, that hadn't been as bad as when they were ten years old and Earl Keys came into their mother's life. He'd convinced her that he'd make a good home for her and her boys. The truth was, Keys only wanted free laborers for his rough-stock business. Every summer both he and Wyatt had worked the rodeo circuit. During the school year, they'd lived on the man's Arizona ranch, but the work hadn't been any easier. Just as soon as the two had turned eighteen, they were gone.

No, neither Randell nor Keys were the best examples of what a father should be. Dylan had no doubt he'd inherited a few bad genes. He'd traveled the circuit and he was damn good at whatever he tried, starting out calf roping with Wyatt. Later, he'd discovered the excitement of bull riding. And the money for his talent and all the endorsements hadn't been bad, either. He was somebody. Then.

He rubbed his leg. Now he was a cripple.

A knock sounded on his bedroom door, then it opened. Brenna stepped just inside. She'd changed into a pair of jeans and blouse that had his juices flowing once again.

"Are you hungry?" she asked. "Or you going to stay in here all night and pout?"

"I'm not pouting," he insisted. "I'm just tired."

She came farther into the room. "You're in good shape. And your stamina has increased, so we can go longer, starting tomorrow."

"What if I don't want to go longer?"

She crossed her arms. "Look, Dylan, we agreed to a

work schedule. If I let you slide now, you'll never get back on your feet. If you're worried about what happened with the cramps, we can work on that.''

This woman was unbelievable. ''I can handle the cramps.'' *It's you I can't seem to handle,* he thought silently.

''Good, because more than likely they'll return. But I can help. There's the whirlpool bath and I can give you a massage.''

He tensed. Oh yeah, that was going to help a lot.

Brenna just stood there for a few more moments.

''Is there something else you want?'' he asked.

''Staying closed up in here isn't good for you, Dylan. Not when you're used to having people around.''

''I don't have a problem with it.''

''As your therapist, I do. Your sister-in-law called and asked if you want to come up to the house for dinner.''

Oh boy, the whole family all at once. He thought about Wyatt and the way he'd handled things earlier.

''If you are worried about the children, I know little Kelly would love to get to know you better.''

''I'm not good with kids.''

''Kelly is female. No matter what her age, I bet you can have her charmed in minutes.'' Brenna wrinkled her nose and Dylan knew she was trying to hide a smile.

''If I'm so good with the ladies, how come it hasn't worked on you?''

Her easy laughter filled the room. ''I don't think you've been trying to charm me, only drive me away. Besides, I'm not a lady. I'm your therapist.''

Ooh, she was definitely a lady. ''Just out of curiosity, what would it take to get your…attention?''

''More than sweet words…or a cocky smile. I have three brothers, and they've inherited a bit of the blarney along with their Irish genes." She sobered. "Besides, I learned a long time ago to believe only half of what men say, and the other half is probably exaggerated."

"Whoa, someone must have done you wrong, lady." He scooted to the edge of the bed and placed his legs on the floor. "Who was he? Want me to go beat him up?"

A sadness transformed her face. "His name was Jason. And you can't beat him up...he's dead." She started to leave, when Dylan reached out and grabbed her arm. She pulled away as tears formed in her eyes.

"Look, I'm sorry. I didn't know." The urge to take her into his arms and hold her was overwhelming.

"It's okay." She moved toward the door. "I guess if you aren't going to your brother's for dinner then I better fix you something."

He shook his head. "No, don't cook, Brenna. We're going to supper at Wyatt's."

"I'll help you get there," she said, "but it would be better if you go to dinner on your own."

"Look, for the past week we've been living in pretty close quarters. And it's been hard to stay out of each other's business, much less their space. I've let you handle me at will, strap me in contraptions, and cause me considerable pain. Now, I'd say you owe me. Please, go with me."

She hesitated. "Okay, but don't think you're going to get your way all the time."

He wanted his way, all right. With her. "I'll take what I can get." He got to his feet. "Give me ten minutes to shower." Using his crutches, he grabbed some underwear and a pair of jeans from the bureau drawer.

"You be sure to use the bench in the tub," she warned.

"Or what? You're coming in and joining me?" He grinned. "Maybe that's not such a bad idea."

He watched her blush, but she didn't back down. "Be careful, remember I can hurt you."

He wasn't thinking pain, only pleasure as he headed off to the shower, a cool one. And for the first time in a long while, it was good to feel alive.

Fifteen minutes later they were both seated in one of the golf carts that belonged to the Mustang Valley Guest Ranch. With Brenna behind the wheel, they headed up to the main house. That was the easy part. The three steps to the porch were much more of a challenge to Dylan.

"You're getting to be pretty good with those crutches," Brenna said.

"Now, who's trying to charm who?" he asked, trying to relax his labored breathing.

"If that's what it takes, I'll do my part."

He smiled, enjoying the easiness between them. "Just how far will you go, Ms. Brenna?"

Even under the porch light, he could see she was flustered, but before she could give a retort the door opened and Kelly appeared. The child looked a little apprehensive, then relaxed seeing Brenna. "Hi, Unca Dylan," she said. "Hi, Brenna."

"Hello, Kelly," Brenna said, and she pulled open the screen door allowing Dylan to go in first. Then she followed.

Dylan's gaze swept around the huge sunny-yellow kitchen. There were pine cabinets and white-tiled countertops. At the stainless-steel stove, his sister-in-law stood cooking. His brother had always talked about having a home. It looked as if he'd gotten his wish.

Maura turned and smiled. "Dylan and Brenna, I'm so glad you both came."

"Thank you for inviting us," Brenna said.

Maura walked over to greet them, surprising Dylan with a hug. Then she stood back and gave him the once-over. "Well, look at you, Dylan, getting around so well." She turned to Brenna. "Thank you for helping him."

"Oh, Dylan is the one who did the work," she insisted. "I only gave him a little push now and then."

"Using a bulldozer," Dylan said, and they all laughed.

The sound of voices drew their attention to the doorway where Wyatt and seven-year-old Jeff walked into the room. He and Wyatt weren't identical twins, Dylan thought, struck once again by their differences, but they were pretty close, with the same height and build. Their hair color was the same, but their eyes were different—his brother's were blue while his were more gray. Wyatt was the more sensible one. Dylan had always been attracted to trouble.

The young boy's face lit up. "Wow, Dad, Uncle Dylan came."

Wyatt smiled. "Yes, son, I'd say he did." He walked up to Dylan. "Glad you could make it, bro."

"I didn't have much choice," Dylan lied as he leaned on his crutches. "This was the only way to get a taste of Maura's meat loaf. You've certainly bragged about it enough."

"Well, come and sit down," Wyatt coaxed. "Dinner shouldn't be too long. Would you like something to drink? Soda? Iced tea? Milk?"

"Iced tea sounds good."

"I'll get it." Jeff ran to the refrigerator, then came

back with a full glass. "Uncle Dylan, Dad said you're the best bull rider in the world."

A sadness moved through him, but he pushed it aside and smiled at his nephew. "Well, I had won the national championship, but someone else won the title this year."

"I told Benny Roberts you did, but he said that I'm lyin' 'cause you aren't really my uncle."

A strange protectiveness came over Dylan. "I guess you just have to prove him wrong. As soon as I locate my things, I'll dig up one of my championship buckles and you can show him."

"Oh, wow!" His eyes rounded. "Can I, really?"

Dylan ruffled the boy's hair. "Yes, you really can."

A smiling Jeff went to his seat across the table, next to Kelly. The little girl looked like her mother, pretty as a picture. When he winked at her, her face lit up with a smile, and a funny feeling circled Dylan's heart.

Brenna leaned toward him. "I think you got yourself a couple of new fans here." She looked him in the eye and whispered, "You've still got it, Dylan 'The Devil' Gentry."

Chapter Three

Two hours later, Wyatt walked Brenna and Dylan out to the porch. She noticed he was careful not to hover too close to his brother, letting him move by himself. Although tired, Dylan seemed to want to show off and made easy work of getting down the steps and into the golf cart.

"Thank Maura again for the great meal," Dylan said.

"Anytime," Wyatt said. "And if you'll let me know where your national championship buckle is, I could get it."

"Impossible. It's in my trailer and that's parked in Arizona."

Wyatt shook his head. "No, it's here," he said. "So is Cheyenne Gold."

Dylan tensed. "You brought my trailer and horse here?"

Wyatt glanced at Brenna, then back at his brother, and nodded. "Yeah. You spent so much time in the hospital, and since you were coming here anyway... I thought

you might need your things close by. No sense you pay-
ing a fortune to store your trailer and board your horse.
Here it's free."

Brenna got in the cart, feeling more than the January
chill. There was new tension between the brothers.

"We should get back," she suggested. "You two can
hash this out when it's warmer. Wyatt, thank Maura
again." She pressed her foot on the pedal and they shot
off down the path.

Once at the cottage, Dylan got out without her help
and went up the single step with ease. Inside, he started
toward the bedroom, but Brenna caught up with him.

"Dylan, why don't you watch television out here?
The screen is bigger. We could put a movie in the
VCR."

"I don't feel like a movie."

"Then stay and talk?" She should keep out of this
situation, but this situation could interfere with her patient's recovery. "I can fix some coffee."

"I know what you're trying to do, Brenna, but it isn't
going to work. I'm mad as hell. So let me be."

She took hold of his arm and got a fierce look as his
silver-blue eyes locked on her.

Somehow she managed to find her voice. "No. Not
until you tell me what was so bad that it ruined the end
of an enjoyable evening with your family."

"I didn't ruin it, my brother did."

Brenna watched as he started to pace a path to the
door then back again. "Tell me what he did that was so
terrible."

"What Wyatt has always done for the past thirty-one
years—try to run my life. He's older than me by five
minutes, and believe me, he has let me know it all our
lives. He's always felt he knows what's best for me. Just

like my coming to the ranch. I agreed to stay here, only until I recovered from my injuries. But he still couldn't leave things alone. It was his idea to get a therapist. I never wanted one. I just wanted to be left alone.

"Now he thinks he had the right to drag my trailer and horse here. Without asking me, I might add. He's just looking for a way to keep me here permanently."

Why did Dylan's words hurt so much? Brenna had known from the beginning that he didn't want a therapist. Over the past week, he'd gotten past that and had accepted her, but hearing the bitterness in his voice now she wasn't so sure. Her own anger flared. She'd be damned if she'd stay where she wasn't wanted.

"You're right, Dylan," she agreed. "Your brother had no right to push you into anything you didn't want. At least one of your problems can be easily solved."

He cocked an eyebrow. "Which one's that?"

Her chest was tight. "Your therapist. I'll have my bags packed and be gone in thirty minutes."

He had blown it big-time.

Dylan knocked on Brenna's bedroom door, but she didn't answer. He knocked again. "Brenna, can we talk?"

No answer.

"Please, Bren. You misunderstood. Open the door and let me explain."

No answer.

He couldn't let her leave, not like this, not at all. He tried the door. It was unlocked. He pushed it open slightly to notice a suitcase on the bed and Brenna placing her clothes inside. "Brenna, will you stop? I don't want you to leave."

She didn't look up. "You said you didn't want me."

"I was only angry with Wyatt for how he'd manipulated me. How he's always been able to get me to do what he wants."

"I don't think he put you on top of that bull, or caused your accident."

"Of course he didn't. But it's a fact that he wanted me here. He wanted me as his partner in this ranch, wanted me to meet the Randells and become part of one big happy family."

She paused and glared at him. "And you want me to sympathize with you for what again?"

"Okay, so it isn't a capital offense. But he won't butt out of my life."

"It's called being part of a family," she retorted. "Deal with it, Gentry. Not everything is always about you. Don't you know that your brother loves you? He's trying to help you the only way he knows how. And all you've done is to get angry and be disagreeable."

"I agree," he admitted.

"And blame everyone else for your misfortune," she continued, not hearing him.

"Hey, I said I agree."

"You may be used to getting everyone's attention while you're perched on a bull, Dylan Gentry, but there are others to consider now."

She had scraped off another layer of his hide. "What do you want?" he asked. "My blood? I said you're right."

She stared at him. "I am?"

"Yes. I've been a rotten bastard. Hard to live with and worse to deal with." He sank down to the edge of the bed and looked at her. "Now, will you stay? Will you help me change? Help me walk again?"

Brenna was caught off guard by his sudden change.

But from day one this man had had a tendency of doing just that…and more. If she was smart, she'd take this opportunity to get far, far away. But she couldn't. She knew she could help him get back on his feet, help give him back a life. Hopefully, it wouldn't be on the back of a bull.

"What about your brother?" she asked. "I think you two need to sit down and work this out."

"We will," he promised. "So, you'll stay and continue my therapy?"

Brenna told herself that it was only for the money, for her baby. "I'll stay."

He grinned at her and she nearly melted to the floor. She was in deep trouble if she didn't find a way to shield her heart from this man.

Early mornings had been Dylan's time. Over the past ten days he'd been pushing himself as hard as he could with the weights and on the parallel bars. In ten days, he'd not only changed his attitude but increased his strength. He had more energy now, more stamina.

Brenna tried to hold him back, warning him that he could do damage if he rushed it. But he wasn't quitting until he was on his feet. On the parallel bars, with Brenna's close attention, and the gait belt for safety, he'd managed to put weight on his bad leg and hold it. The pain was bad, but worth it as he took that first, shaky step. He still needed more strength in his legs…a lot more, and he was getting tired of waiting. That's why he worked overtime with the leg weights.

He'd also talked with Wyatt, apologized for his behavior, but asked his brother to check with him before making any more decisions about his life. Dylan wanted to make those on his own.

With his progress, he was thinking it might be possible to get back on the circuit. He missed the travel, the crowds and yeah, the female attention... He thought about how long it had been since he had kissed and caressed a woman, had one in his bed. He closed his eyes and Brenna's face came into focus. He released a groan and sat up at the bench. It infuriated him that his reaction to her was so strong. He wiped the sweat from his face and got up to head to the shower. A long, cold one.

A soft knock sounded on the door. "Come in," he called.

The door opened and little Kelly poked her head in. "Hi, Unca Dylan. You busy?" She smiled brightly.

He found he'd looked forward to her visits before heading off to school.

"Not for my favorite niece." The cute blonde wasn't a blood relative, but Wyatt had adopted both Jeff and Kelly when he married their mother. That was close enough for him.

She giggled. "I brought you something." She held up a picture that looked like a bunch of scribbling.

"That's very nice."

"It's Mommy, Daddy and Jeff and me." She pointed off to the side. "That's our house. It's for you to hang up. That's so we can be with you all the time."

"That's real nice, Kelly. I'll tape your drawing to the refrigerator so I can look at it whenever I want."

She walked up to him and whispered, "I know a secret, too."

"You do?" The child's eyes were wide with excitement. He played along. "You want to tell me?"

She shrugged. "You have to cross your heart and

promise not to tell." She ran her small hand over her coat.

He did the same. "I cross my heart."

"Mommy has a baby in her tummy."

Dylan didn't expect to feel the rush of emotion. Was it true or just wishful thinking on the child's part? "She does? How do you know?"

She rolled her eyes. "'Cause the pink stick says so. That's how you know."

"Oh." How did a four-year-old know about a pregnancy test?

"Mommy and Daddy were whispering about it in the bathroom. Mommy was cryin', but they were happy tears. And Daddy was kissin' her." She sighed. "They kiss a lot."

No doubt, Dylan thought as a pang of jealousy hit him. "Well, maybe we shouldn't say anything. I think they want to surprise everybody."

Kelly placed a finger against her lips. "I won't tell."

"That's good because if you do, you know what will happen?"

She shook her head, causing her ponytail to swish back and forth.

"The tickle monster will come and grab you." He lifted her onto his lap and began to tickle her ribs, making her giggle. Just then Brenna came into the room.

"Help me," Kelly cried in between fits of laughter. "Unca Dylan won't stop tickling me."

"Is that so? Well, we have to do something about that." Brenna came up behind Dylan on the bench and went after his ribs.

Dylan didn't know how it happened but he was soon the one under attack by both females. He managed to release Kelly and grabbed for Brenna. Somehow she ended up in his lap, her cute little bottom fitting nicely against him. That was when he looked up and saw Wyatt and Maura standing in the doorway.

"Don't let us interrupt…your therapy," Wyatt said.

Brenna felt heat rush to her face, realizing what she was doing. Her behavior was so unprofessional and so unlike her. She scrambled off Dylan's lap. "Wyatt, Maura, please come in."

"You want to help me, bro?" Dylan said. "Seems the girls have outnumbered me."

"Looks like fun, but I'll have to pass." Wyatt glanced at his daughter. "Kelly, you didn't tell us where you went. Your mother was worried."

"Sorry. I brought Unca Dylan a picture." She pointed to the one on the sofa.

"Well, next time tell us when you leave the house."

"'Kay. Am I in trouble?"

Brenna watched as the wide-eyed child looked up at her daddy, her lower lip forming a pout. Kelly was good. Brenna knew because she used to do the same with her father. "Wyatt and Maura, why don't you sit down and I'll make some coffee."

Maura shook her head. "No, thank you. I need to get to work. Besides, I'm off coffee for a while." She glanced up at her husband and smiled. "Come on, Kelly, we need to get going."

The girl took her hand, then smiled back at her uncle before walking off with her parents.

Brenna looked at Dylan. "You two looked thick as thieves."

"That's because we share a secret."

She smiled. "It's great that you and Kelly are getting along so well."

She started to walk away. He reached out and pulled

her onto the weight bench, his strength tumbling her backward. He ended up leaning over her, causing his black hair to fall over his forehead. There was a sexy glint in his eyes. "I bet you want to know what it is."

The pressure of his hard body against hers was far too distracting. "Not really. Now, let me up."

A playful grin appeared across his handsome face, and she knew how he'd gotten his nickname.

"It's different when I have the advantage," he teased.

"Just let me up," she insisted.

He only shifted closer. When his eyes met hers, the mesmerizing silvery-blue gaze ended her futile struggle.

"Aren't you the least bit curious?" he asked.

Brenna suddenly realized that his question had nothing to do with any secret. Unable to stop herself, she gave a surrendering nod. Dylan lowered his head and his lips met hers in a gentle caress. She should have resisted, but she only managed a faint whimper as he began to take tiny nibbles from her lips. Finally his mouth closed over hers, so gently and searchingly, as if he was trying to savor her.

Then without warning, the kiss changed as Dylan ran his tongue over the seam of her lips, teasing and probing until she opened to him. With a groan, he delved inside to taste her. Brenna's body grew aroused and instinctively she moved against him.

"Bren..." He breathed her name, then captured her mouth once again. The kiss was deep and thorough, driving her desire higher and higher. She couldn't think about anything but this man. Suddenly there was a ringing sound.

Dylan drew away with a curse and reached for the cordless phone. "Hello," he growled.

Brenna sat up quickly and tried to pull herself together. She took a calming breath, but nothing eased the anger and shame she felt for her behavior. If she was to continue this job, she had to somehow stay away from Dylan Gentry.

Dylan hung up the phone. "Sorry about the interruption. It was my manager." He reached for her hand as she tried to stand. "Hey, where are you going?"

"I need to fix breakfast." She tried to keep the trembling out of her voice, tried to break his tight grip. "I'd say it was a good thing it happened—the interruption, I mean."

"Now, that's where we disagree," he told her. "I'd say it's a good thing the kiss happened."

Brenna drew back. "No, Dylan. That wasn't a good thing. I'm your therapist."

"I'm also a man and you're a woman and we were both curious about what it would be like if we kissed."

And I'm pregnant with another man's child, she reminded herself. "Okay, so now we know," she relented. "And we can forget about it."

He hesitated a moment, then nodded. "All right. If that's the way you want it. But if you change your mind—"

"This isn't a joke," Brenna interrupted him. "And I'm not going to be one of your conquests." She broke free and took off into the kitchen. How could she so easily have forgotten Jason and jumped into this man's arms?

It wasn't long before Dylan came up behind her. "Look, Brenna, I didn't mean to upset you. I overstepped, but it was only a kiss." There was a long pause, then he spoke again, "And you're wrong, never once have I never thought about you being a...conquest. If you've been reading up about me you would know that I prefer blondes.''

She turned to him and glared, but he was grinning at her. Darn the man. "So you can't handle us feisty red-heads? Too much fire, ah?"

He started to speak, then stopped. "I'm not going to touch that one."

"Chicken," she teased, finally starting to relax.

"You're damn straight. You can cause me a lot of pain."

She smiled this time. "You're learning."

"So we're friends again?" he asked.

"Friends," she agreed, knowing it was a dangerous move.

Dylan leaned on his crutches and studied Brenna's flushed face. He had to admit that he reacted more strongly to her than he wanted...or needed. But the feel of her body against him drove him to do irrational things. And the last thing he needed was to get involved with this woman. She was the type who would be hard to walk away from...and that was all he'd been good at. Except this time he wasn't even able to walk. Yet.

With another look, he noticed there were blue shadows under her eyes. Dammit, he didn't want to worry about her, either. "Are you okay?"

She nodded. "I'm just a little tired."

No wonder, when she wasn't getting much sleep. He'd heard her moving around before dawn. "That's because you're up before the sun."

She opened the refrigerator. "I'm used to little sleep." She took out the bacon and began placing strips in the warming skillet.

"Bren, I don't want to argue with you. I'm just concerned you're working yourself too hard."

"I'm used to hard work," she insisted. "I had two part-time jobs in college, while I was carrying a full load of classes. Before that, I lived on my parents' ranch. Being a girl didn't mean my chores were any easier. Believe me, I can handle this job, Dylan." Her gaze met his. "Unless you have any complaints."

Dylan sighed. Only that she was too pretty not to notice, that he wanted to kiss that sassy mouth of hers again and again.

He shook away the thought. "Not a one, Bren. You've convinced me."

"Well, praise be, I think you're catching on."

"Okay, so I'm a slow learner."

"I'd say you learn pretty fast. Your progress has been remarkable."

He waved his hand. "Let's not talk about me anymore." He smiled. "Want to know my secret?"

"I thought you said you were good at keeping secrets. If you tell me then it's no longer a secret." She got two plates down from the cupboard, took out flatware from the drawer and carried it to the table.

He followed her. "It's good news."

"So, keep it to yourself." She went back into the kitchen.

He wasn't listening. "Okay, I'll give you a hint. Someone is pregnant."

Chapter Four

Brenna's heart skipped a beat, then began racing. Oh God, how did he find out? "How did you know?" she gasped.

Dylan's smile widened. "I wasn't sure at first. You never know how reliable kids are. But when Wyatt and Maura walked in here earlier I was pretty sure it was true. I mean, Maura had a glow about her—"

"Maura?" Brenna interrupted, confused as to what he was saying.

"Yeah, she's pregnant."

Brenna sank against the counter with the unexpected reprieve. "Maura's pregnant?"

"Is there an echo in here?" He frowned. "Isn't that what I just said? That was Kelly's big secret. Seems she overheard her parents talking about a pink stick and a baby. And seeing the grin on my brother's face, I'd say it was true. You knew, too?"

"Huh…yeah," she lied, trying to be convincing.

"Just don't let on, okay? They probably wanted to wait until the time was right to tell everyone."

"I can keep a secret."

Her mouth twitched.

"All right, you caught me at a weak moment," he admitted.

Dylan wasn't talking about the secret anymore. Brenna glanced away, but was lured back by his infectious smile. Then that smile disappeared and his blue eyes searched hers. She knew that he was thinking about the kiss, too. Brenna tried to erase it from her mind, but she could still feel the imprint of his mouth on hers, still taste him. Her chest suddenly tightened, her breasts grew heavy and sensitive. Dylan noticed it too as he shifted his gaze to her T-shirt. His bold inspection instantly caused her nipples to harden.

She drew a quick breath. "Are you hungry?" she asked and immediately regretted her choice of words. "I mean, you should have some protein."

Dylan was trying hard not to break his promise, but Brenna Farren was a tempting woman. Damn, he never should have kissed her in the first place. She was his therapist, for God's sake. She was the one who was going to get him back on the circuit. So that meant he had to find a way to curb his desire for her. But there was no way he could change things back to the way they were before, before he got an intriguing sample. He started to answer her but was interrupted by a knock on the door.

"Sure is busy around here this morning." With the aid of his crutches, he headed across the room. He pulled open the door expecting to find Wyatt. Instead, there was an older man standing on the porch. He was in his mid-

sixties with a head of thick gray hair. His face was
weathered with lines, especially around the eyes.

"Good mornin'." He smiled. "I apologize for both-
ering you so early, but Wyatt said you'd be up." He
offered his hand. "I'm Hank Barrett. I wanted to stop
by and welcome you to San Angelo."

Dylan was caught off guard as he took the man's
hand. "I'm Dylan."

"I guessed that. You look too much like your brother
not to be." Barrett's smile faded. "We're all sorry to
hear about your accident, but I'm glad to see you're
doin' so well." He fiddled with the black Stetson in his
hands. "Do you mind if I speak with you a moment?"

Dylan nodded and moved aside. "Come in."

"Thank you," Hank said as he stepped into the cottage and glanced around at all the equipment. "I see
you're busy, so I won't keep you long," he said. Then
he spotted Brenna in the kitchen area and grinned. "Is
that you, Brenna Farren?"

Brenna came forward. She wiped her hands on her
sweats. "Hello, Mr. Barrett."

"Oh, I think you're old enough now to call me Hank.
Aren't you a sight for these old peepers." He examined
her closely. "Land sakes, I haven't seen you since before you took off for college."

"I graduated last summer."

"I know. Your daddy has been shoutin' the news to
everybody. He's sure happy his girl is home."

Dylan watched her blush.

"I'm happy to be here, too."

Hank looked at Dylan. "She must be good at her job
if she got you on your feet."

"Brenna's a real slave driver," Dylan said, finding it
easy to talk to the man.

"*Someone* has to get you to do your therapy," she insisted.

"Sounds like you're both what each other needs." The older man glanced back and forth between the two. "Look, I didn't mean to interrupt you. I just wanted to stop by and invite the two of you to supper this week-end."

Dylan tensed. He'd bet his favorite pair of chaps that he'd be seeing the Randell brothers at this supper. "I don't know if that's such a good idea."

"Look, Dylan. I don't want to put any pressure on you. But you've been pretty much holed up here the past month. Thought you'd like a night out. And maybe you're just a little curious about Chance, Cade, Travis and Jared."

"Not really," Dylan said, realizing he was curious...a little.

Hank nodded, but didn't look as if he was about to give up. "Then how about you come as a neighbor accepting an invitation from another neighbor? I doubt the boys are going to force themselves on you. I think right now they're more interested in your ability to ride a bull than the fact that you're a blood relation."

"I'm not much interested in any part of Jack Randell's life."

A wide grin appeared on Hank's face. "Well, you see, you already have something in common with them after all. Chance, Cade and Travis want no part of Jack, either."

Dylan glanced at Brenna. She gave him a hopeful look. "I could drive, and if it gets to be too much for you, I could bring you home."

What did he have to lose? He turned to Hank. "What time?"

The older man sighed. "Anytime after five will be fine. With my housekeeper, Ella, it's hard to tell when everything gets put on the table." He looked at Brenna. "As I remember correctly, your mother, Maggie, was a pretty good cook. I bet you inherited some of her talent."

"I'm not bad," she said. "I would love to bring something."

"That sounds great. See you both Saturday." With a wave, he walked out and closed the door behind him.

Brenna turned to Dylan. "Well, you are a surprise, Gentry."

He shrugged. "I'm just keeping my promise."

She folded her arms over her chest. "And which promise is that?"

"That I would work on changing my attitude if you'd stay."

"So you're okay with the possibility of meeting your brothers?"

"Whoa, there." He raised a hand. "I only have one brother and that's Wyatt. As far as I'm concerned, these Randells are just neighbors." He wasn't about to admit to her that he was curious to meet them, too.

"Well, that's a start," Brenna said, and headed back to the kitchen.

He followed her. "What is that supposed to mean?"

"Nothing. Just that you're at least meeting them. The Randells are pretty nice people." She smiled. "But then you'll find that out all by yourself."

Three days later, Brenna drove Dylan to the Circle B Ranch. She used the twenty-minute trip to fill him in on

the history of the Circle B and how Hank recently had
turned the running of the ranch over to the brothers.

Now it was part of the family business. Hank's Circle
B, Chance and Joy's ranch, Cade and Abby's ranch,
along with a small section of Jared and Dana's property
that all met together at the valley, were all part of the
Mustang Valley Guest Ranch. Even Wyatt's place was
included in the package, expanding the operation with a
working cattle ranch. At this time of year the place was
closed until spring. The Randells loved having the
chance to spend time with their families.

Brenna looked across the seat at Dylan. He hadn't said
a word since he got into the truck. No doubt tonight was
going to be difficult for him.

"You know, the Randells aren't going to push you
into anything. I think they just want to get to meet you.
Like Hank said, they're in awe of the fact that you're a
world-champion bull rider."

"I guess I should have brought my buckles," he said
sarcastically.

"Dylan, don't be this way. The Randells are trying to
reach out to you. Remember, they were as shocked as
you must have been at finding out they had three half
brothers."

"You're right." He released a long breath. "I'll be-
have."

She turned off the highway onto a gravel road and
headed past the rows of white-fenced pastures where cattle grazed in the high grass. They drove under the
wrought-iron archway that read Circle B Ranch. Soon
outbuildings came into view, a barn, then a large two-
story gray house with white shutters.

Brenna continued past a row of cars and trucks until
she reached a long white building with the name over

the door reading, Circle B Chuckwagon. She parked and turned off the engine.

"Hanks says now that the family is so big, they have to eat their meals here in the guest-ranch dining hall when they all get together."

Dylan remained stone-faced. "I guess we should get this over with." He raised the door handle and started to get out.

"Wait, Dylan." Brenna stopped him. "I'm telling you right now, I don't want you to have a good time. If that starts to happen, you let me know and I'll get you the heck out of the there."

"Very funny," he said, but she could see he was fighting a smile.

She released his arm, climbed out and went around to his door. He didn't need her help, but she was standing nearby just in case.

Dylan eased out, set his crutches under his arms before heading for the entrance, where he was met with the sound of laughter and children's voices coming from inside.

Wyatt came out to greet them. "It's about time you showed up." He glanced at Brenna. "He giving you trouble?"

"Nothing I can't handle," she said.

"Well, you're officially off duty for the evening. I'll take care of this guy. I want you to enjoy yourself."

Brenna knew the Randells, but not well. They had all been ahead of her in school. She reminded herself being invited was part of her job. Wyatt could have brought his brother, but she doubted Dylan would have come if she hadn't offered to take him back home whenever he wanted to leave. She took her rice-and-mushroom casserole out of the truck and followed the men inside. Already several people had surrounded Wyatt and Dylan. She paused and decided to stay back. He needed to deal with this himself.

Brenna started across the pine floor, skirting several children and the long tables with high-back chairs, toward the kitchen area. A stainless-steel counter already held several dishes of food, including a huge bin of fried chicken.

She set down her dish and started to turn around when she heard her name.

"Well, if it isn't little Brenna Farren."

She looked up to find the Circle B's housekeeper, Ella. She was a tall, big-boned woman dressed in a plaid blouse and black jeans. Her gray hair was cut short and combed back from her handsome face.

"Hello, Ella. How are you?"

The housekeeper gave her a big hug. "I'm the same, but you've grown into a real beauty. I heard you were home. I bet your mama is happy about that."

Brenna nodded. "Although I haven't been able to spend much time with Mom and Dad. I've been working."

Ella raised an eyebrow. "I know those Gentry men are easy on the eyes, but take the time to get home and see your folks."

"I promise. It's just that Dylan needs most of my attention these first few weeks."

Ella glanced at the crowd across the room. "Looks like he's standing on his own pretty good."

Brenna couldn't deny that, and he was growing stronger day by day.

A short time later, Joy and Abby Randell came up to Brenna and introduced themselves. Joy was married to the oldest brother, Chance. They had a daughter, Katie

Rose, and a three-month-old son, Dane. Abby was married to the second oldest brother, Cade. They had two boys, a ten-year-old, Brandon, and a two-year-old, James Henry.

The next to arrive was the pretty, dark-haired Josie Randell. She was married to the youngest brother, Travis. They had a little girl nearly two years old, Elissa Mae. Josie was also Hank's biological daughter who he'd only learned about a few years ago.

Another arrival to the group was Dana Shayne Trager. She was married to Jared, the first of Jack's illegitimate sons. He'd been the one who had a picture of Sally Gentry and Jack Randell together. Dana had a five-year-old son, Evan, and another baby on the way. Finally Maura joined the group of women and made her announcement that she and Wyatt were expecting a baby in September. The Randell family was certainly growing.

Brenna couldn't resist any longer and asked to hold Dane. Joy relinquished her tiny son, who looked so much like his father, Chance. Surprisingly, he also looked like his uncle Dylan. Brenna couldn't help wondering who her baby would resemble. Would he be the image of Jason?

The biggest problem was how to explain her situation to her family. Would they accept the news of their first grandchild with enthusiasm? How would Dylan take it? Would he let her continue being his therapist? He had made so much progress in the past month. The last thing she wanted was for him to quit. She glanced across the room and saw him talking with the Randell brothers. He was making a different kind of progress now. And he seemed to be fitting in just fine.

The other ladies in the group noticed it too. ''Would

you look at that," Joy said in amazement. "All six of them. The brothers are finally together."

Dylan sat at the table as Chance, Cade and Travis took turns telling him about their childhood. Dylan quickly learned how hard it had been on all of them—that being a legitimate son of Jack Randell hadn't been easy. Although Hank had taken them in, they hadn't had an easy time. They'd had to do a lot to convince people they weren't like their father.

"Our lives must sound pretty boring compared to yours," Travis said. "I bet you miss the rodeo."

"Yeah, I miss it," Dylan admitted, absently rubbing his leg. "But as you can see, I got pretty banged up. I still have a long way to go before I can compete again."

"So you're plannin' on going back to the circuit?" Travis asked.

"I'd like to," Dylan admitted. "I don't know anything else."

Wyatt interrupted. "I've been trying to get Dylan to stay and be my partner."

"I'm not ready to retire yet," Dylan insisted. "If I continue the therapy and if the doctor releases me, I figure I have a good year where I can still be competitive."

Cade laughed. "Boy, can tell you're single." He was the tallest of all the brothers, and the darkest, with his brown eyes and black hair. He was a part-time rancher and financial adviser. "Abby would kill me if I tried anything that dangerous."

"As would Joy and Josie," Chance added with a grin. He was a quarter-horse breeder and trainer. "But I wouldn't have it any other way. The right woman excites me more than sitting on an ugly bull for the thrill of an eight-second ride. No offense, Dylan.''

"None taken," Dylan said. "Everyone needs to do what they love."

"You're right," Jared said. "I get to be a carpenter. Chance, you have your horses. Cade, you play the market and Travis still works in computer security. And even Wyatt's got his rough-stock business." He smiled. "I'd say we're all following our hearts."

Dylan nodded in agreement, but he wasn't like these guys. They all had homes and families...a special woman. He'd never wanted any part of that. So why was he envying these men?

Dylan was grateful when his attention was drawn to questions from the kids. He answered them the best he could and promised to bring his championship buckles the next time. Feeling a little closed in, he looked around, hoping to find Brenna. He finally spotted her standing with the other women. She turned and his breath caught. She had a baby cuddled against her breast. The tiny infant's fingers were latched on to one of hers. Brenna was beaming as she cooed at the child.

Then, as if she sensed someone was watching her, she raised her head and their eyes met. Blood pulsed through his body, causing a searing heat to pool low in his gut.

Chance said something, but Dylan couldn't make it out as he tried to focus.

"I think the man's distracted," Chance said, and laughter broke out. "He hasn't heard a word we're saying."

"What?" Dylan asked. "Did you say something?"

"Nothing important," Chance commented, smiling.

"Well, I have some important news," Wyatt said. "Maura is pregnant."

Wyatt got slaps on the back and congratulations from the group. Dylan was happy for his brother, too.

Dylan's attention was drawn back to Brenna. Damn. She looked like a natural with the baby. That alone should be reason enough to stay far away from her. Easier said than done, especially since he'd kissed her. All he could think about was doing it again. Not a good idea when he was determined to go back on the circuit.

"Admit it, the Randells aren't so bad," Brenna coaxed as she drove them back to the cottage.

Dylan kept his gaze on the glow from the truck's headlights lighting the dark road. "No, they aren't, but that doesn't mean I'm going to fit in here."

"Dylan, Wyatt didn't fit in at first, either. You should give yourself some time, get to know them."

"All right, I will. But that's not going to change the fact that I'm going back to the circuit. If I remember correctly, that was how you convinced me to let you keep the job. You promised to get me on my feet. Are you going back on your word?"

She stiffened. "No. I'm not going back on my word." She turned on to the driveway, then drove past the main house to the cottage.

She shut off the engine. "It just seems crazy to me that you're risking your life for—"

"Brenna, it's my life," he interrupted and clasped his hand on her arm before she could get out of the car. "And that makes it not your concern."

It was too dark to see her face, but he inhaled her scent, reminding him of her softness, her kiss.

"Fine," she whispered. "Like you said, my job will be over once you get back on your feet." Brenna climbed out of the cab and slammed the door. She came around to help him, but he'd already gotten out. Seeing he didn't need her help, she walked up to the porch and went inside the cottage. By the time Dylan got there, Brenna was already in her room with the door closed. He didn't blame her, he wasn't fit company for anyone.

Brenna paced her small room, trying to relieve some of her anger. Damn that man. Hadn't she learned her lesson? Dylan Gentry was a bull rider. He wanted life with the rodeo rather than any family.

No more attempts to try to save a man who didn't want to be saved, she vowed. Jason had taught her a bitter lesson. She wasn't important enough to him to stop his dangerous lifestyle.

She lay down on the bed and placed her hand over her slightly rounded stomach. Tonight, seeing how protective the Randell men were with their wives made her feel more alone than ever. She knew none of the couples had had an easy time finding love, but eventually it had all worked out, with happy endings for each one of them.

Guess that wasn't meant to be for Brenna and her child. Jason was gone and her baby was without a father. And soon she wouldn't be able to hide the fact that she was pregnant. Her parents had to be told. She prayed for a little more time, a few more weeks, just so she could finish her job here. But she couldn't stay away from her parents much longer. And Brenna knew the second her mother saw her, she would know something was up. Brenna didn't want to see the disappointment in her eyes.

There was a knock on the door. She pulled down her bulky sweater and sat up. "Come in."

The door swung open and Dylan stood in the doorway. "I want to apologize. I shouldn't have gotten angry with you."

"And maybe I shouldn't have pushed you. You did a good thing going to the Circle B tonight. I know it made Wyatt happy."

"I don't think it takes much these days to make my brother happy. Maura and the kids and the ranch are doing a pretty good job of that."

Brenna couldn't help but see the obvious love between the couple. "Yeah, it shows."

Dylan took one step inside, then sat down on the end of the bed. Brenna started to protest, but they had lived in such close quarters during the past weeks, it would be silly to get prissy now.

"Were you that happy with…Jason?"

Startled by the question, her gaze darted to his. But she couldn't lie. "No. Maybe that's the reason I see how special Wyatt and Maura's relationship is."

"It seems like an epidemic around here. Every couple tonight was gushing. I felt like I was intruding." He looked at her. "How did you feel?"

She nodded. "The same," she admitted. "I even saw sparks between Ella and Hank."

"Damn, I thought it was just me." They both laughed, then Dylan sobered. "I need to get out more."

She smiled. "Shows you're on the mend and getting impatient. Besides tonight, the only place you've gone is to the doctor's and Wyatt's."

"I can't drive."

"This ranch is pretty big. You can go out with your brother. He'd probably get a kick out of showing you around. You have a golf cart at your disposal. Why not surprise him tomorrow?"

"I think I will." He glanced back at her. "You look tired. Why don't you take tomorrow off?"

"Whoa, I'm the one who says when you can stop your therapy." She stood. "You're at a critical stage, Dylan."

"Bren, I'm not slacking off. You know how much I want to get back on my feet. Look at me." He stood and put weight on his injured leg. "I've been adding more and more weight every day." He wasn't even leaning on the crutches. "Maybe I can start using a cane."

She knew he'd advanced way ahead with his therapy. "Why don't we wait until you see Dr. Morris?" He nodded then went to reach for his crutches and lost his balance. Brenna tried to help but they both ended up on the bed.

He raised his head and grinned. "Thanks for the help, Bren. But in the future, I can handle it."

Brenna needed to keep the situation light, but she couldn't think when his body was pressed into hers, his heat burning every inch of her. She swallowed hard. "It's a reflex. I don't usually let my patients fall." His face was inches from hers, his breath caressed her cheek. Somehow she managed to push him off of her and stood, offering her hand.

He waved her off. "It's been a while since I needed help getting out of bed."

Brenna felt her cheeks flame, remembering that first morning and Dylan's nude body. She stood back and watched him get to his feet, knowing she wasn't going to be needed much longer. "You've come a long way, Dylan. You've got to be proud of your progress."

"I'll be much happier when I walk out of here under my own power." He grabbed his crutches and headed to the door, then turned around. "Brenna, thanks for going with me tonight."

She nodded. "You're welcome. I had a good time."

"I could see that when you were holding the baby."

She glanced away. "They're hard to resist."

He stood there as seconds ticked by, making Brenna aware of the small room. "I'm sorry that things didn't work out between you and Jason." He paused again. "You deserve better."

Brenna didn't know how to respond, but Dylan didn't seem to expect a response as he left. She sank onto the bed. "I don't know if I do, but my child does."

Chapter Five

The next morning, Dylan was up by six-thirty and drove to the main house. Careful to balance his weight on his good leg, he climbed out of the golf cart, and reached back into the cart for one crutch. He was determined to start walking again. Hopping around on one foot wasn't getting him anywhere. The doctor had said it was all right to put weight on the injured leg, just be sensible.

Using the railing, Dylan made his way up the four steps to the back porch. He shifted the crutch under his right arm, then placed his foot on the floor. Adding some weight, he tested the leg's strength. It felt stiff but not too bad. With a slow, limping gait, he made his way to the door and knocked, then stepped into the warm kitchen.

That's where he found Wyatt and Maura standing at the stove locked in a loving embrace. His brother's arms were wrapped around his petite wife as he gazed down at her. The intense look exchanged between the two was sizzling…and intimate. Finally the couple noticed their intruder, but it was he who was embarrassed.

"Hey, don't you two ever stop?" he said. "Remember, there are innocent children around."

"Not at this hour," Wyatt said. "Only annoying brothers."

"Stop it, Wyatt," Maura declared. She was dressed in a pair of dark pleated trousers and a white silky blouse. Her long blond hair lying against her shoulder was a little mussed, no doubt by Wyatt's hands.

Escaping her husband's hold, she came to greet him with a hug. "Dylan, you are always welcome here. Anytime. Please, come sit down, you're just in time for breakfast."

"Now, that's what I call a welcome." He smiled brightly. "Thank you, Maura," Dylan said as he limped his way across the room.

"Hey, don't look now but you're missing a crutch," Wyatt pointed out.

Dylan collapsed in the chair. "It's outside in the cart. I thought it was time I try out this bum leg and see how things go." He thanked Maura as she set two mugs of coffee on the table.

His brother sat down across from him. "How does it feel?"

"Not too bad, but I'm not planning on running a marathon, either."

Wyatt nodded but held Dylan's gaze. "Did you just stop by to show off, or was there something else that brought you out so early?"

He shrugged. "Is there anything wrong with a brother coming by to visit?" He smiled at Maura. "And maybe sharing some breakfast."

"So Brenna threw you out, did she?"

"No. She just *suggested* that I get out of the house for a while. Besides, she hasn't had a day off since she started working with me." Dylan couldn't help but notice how tired Brenna had been looking the past week.

"Oh, man, that's cruel and unusual punishment."

Dylan glared at his brother. "Are you trying to tell me I'm hard to get along with?"

Wyatt's grin widened. "Yeah, you're a real pain, but we love you anyway."

Just then little Kelly came into the room still dressed in pink pajamas. "Unca Dylan!" she cried and ran to hug him. "Are you going to eat breakfast with us?"

He pulled his niece onto his lap. "If it's okay with you."

She nodded. "You can eat here every day if you want."

They all laughed. "I think your mom and dad would get a little tired of seeing me."

"I won't. I love you." Her tiny arms went around his neck in a hug. Dylan's chest grew tight. In the short time he'd known them, both Jeff and Kelly had worked their way into his heart.

"I love you too, darlin'," he confessed. "You want to be my best girl?"

Kelly nodded, then laughed. "I can't. Brenna is your girlfriend."

Dylan was caught off guard. "Honey, Brenna is helping me walk."

"But you like her, don't ya?" Kelly asked.

"Yes," he admitted. More than he should.

"My mommy likes my daddy and they're going to have a baby, maybe you can make a baby with Brenna—"

"Kelly Ann!" Maura interrupted her daughter.

"Honey, it's time for you to get dressed for school. I'll be up in a few minutes to brush your hair."

"But Mommy, I wanna talk to Unca Dylan."

"Later. C'mon," she said, holding out her hand.

"'Kay." Reluctantly the child climbed off Dylan's lap and went to her mother. Maura scooted her out of the room as she sent an apologetic look Dylan's way.

"Sorry," Maura said. "As you can see, children have a pretty vivid imagination."

"Don't I know it," Dylan joked. "You better watch out for that one."

"Why, because she sees something going on between you and Brenna?" Wyatt asked.

Dylan wasn't going to let his brother bait him. "No, because Kelly told me last week she overheard you two talking about a pink stick and a baby in her mommy's tummy."

Maura gasped, her face reddening. "Oh, Wyatt, she must have been listening at the bathroom door. That little stinker."

Wyatt's eyes rolled. "I'm more concerned about what else she's been hearing between us."

The red deepened on Maura's face as she smacked her husband on the arm. "I think you should talk with her."

"Me?" Wyatt choked. "Ah, come on, Maura. You know I can't handle her tears."

"You're such a pushover, and don't think the kids don't know that." Maura walked back to the stove and served up two plates of ham and eggs. She glanced at the clock. "Oh, I better get going. I need to get to the Yellow Rose flower shop. I have a special shipment this morning from the flower wholesaler. The Stanley wedding is this weekend." She looked at Dylan. "Don't be a stranger.'' She kissed Wyatt's cheek. "Don't forget to take Jeff over to the Lazy S so he can spend the day with Evan.''

"Promise.'' Wyatt kissed her again, then let her go.

"Looks like a certain female around here got your number.'' Dylan picked up his fork and began to eat.

Wyatt shrugged. "Hey, there are worse ways to live. Now, tell me what's going on between you and Brenna.''

"Nothing. She's my therapist. That's all.'' He took a bite of ham.

"So you're immune to the fact that you're living with a beautiful redhead?''

Oh, yeah, he'd definitely been aware. "You're the one who hired her. I thought you'd be happy that things are strictly business.''

"Does she have someone else in her life?''

"She did.'' He remembered the sadness in her voice as she spoke of Jason. "That's beside the point. Soon I'll be going back to bull riding, and she'll go on to another job.''

"Let's just say—if you weren't going back and wanted to settle down—could you be interested in Brenna Farren?''

Dylan knew a trick question when he heard one. "Of course. Like you said, she's a beautiful woman. But you know I don't do permanent relationships.'' He needed to change the subject and fast. "Hey, how about showing me around the ranch this morning?''

Wyatt raised an eyebrow. "Really? You want to see the operation?''

"Sure, I want a look at those bulls I'm going to be riding.''

Wyatt grinned. "I got a few young ones that are

promising, but Bud and the crew took the Gentry rough stock to a rodeo in Arizona.''

"Why aren't you with them?"

Wyatt picked up his mug and leaned back in his chair. "That's what's great about being the boss. I've done enough traveling over the years. Besides, I have three good reasons to keep me home—and keep me happy." Then he added. "Make that four with the baby."

Thirty minutes later, Wyatt and Dylan were in the cart and driving to the pens where the rodeo stock were kept. The facility was impressive with top-of-the-line metal fences and pens, along with a new barn where Wyatt kept his champion bucking horses. He had a lot invested in the new business, and with the recent contracts for the coming season, they would show a profit this year.

Next, they went by Dylan's trailer so he could pick up more clothes and some more rodeo trinkets to give to Jeff and Kelly. He also stopped at the barn and checked on his horse. They pulled up right next to the animal's stall. Ignoring the crutch, Dylan got out and grabbed the rail to brace himself as he looked in to see Cheyenne.

"Hey, fella."

The big, golden-yellow chestnut horse whinnied and came to greet him. Dylan stroked the animal's head playfully and at the same time tried to keep his balance, but the horse was too excited. Dylan staggered backward, but Wyatt caught him, then handed him his crutch.

"I guess you can say he's missed you."

Dylan laughed. He knew Cheyenne wasn't going to stop pestering him until he got to run. "I can't give him what he needs—a good run."

Wyatt tried to ease his concerns. "He's out in the

corral most of the day, I bring him in at night. One of the ranch hands takes him for a run every few days. Is there anything else you want us to do?''

Just that Dylan would have liked to be the one to ride him. ''No, looks like you got everything covered.'' He was going to check with Brenna to see when he'd be able to ride Cheyenne himself.

Dylan pulled his cowboy hat down lower. The February wind was frigid as Wyatt continued the tour and drove out to the pasture. Even his sheepskin coat didn't keep out the chill, but it felt wonderful. His brother stopped on a ridge and pointed to a large herd of Herefords grazing in the valley.

Dylan shook his head. ''I can't believe you're in the cattle business.''

''Why? Our paternal grandfather was a very successful cattle rancher.''

Dylan turned away.

''Look, bro, we may not want to acknowledge our biological father, but John Randell had nothing to do with the circumstances of our birth. He was a well respected man around this area and I'm proud to carry on his legacy with the Rocking R. Besides, the cattle business is profitable.'' He looked at Dylan. ''I'm a partner in the Mustang Valley Corporation.''

''Sounds like you and the Randells are pretty tight.'' Dylan found himself envious of their relationship. All his life, it had just been him and his brother.

''Yeah, we've become friends. You saw last night, the brothers have accepted us—you, me and Jared. They didn't have to, either. If you hang around a while, you'll discover their strong sense of family. Something we never had.''

"Well, nothing against the Randells, but that's not going to happen. My life is out on the circuit."

Wyatt nodded. "Okay, but when you do decide to retire, will you think about settling down here? We can split the Rocking R."

"What would I do on a ranch?"

"What you do best," Wyatt said. "Teach bull riding. Open a school. Your name alone would bring people in. And you could help me. You've ridden more bulls than anyone I know. You could probably look at one and know if he's going to be any good on the circuit."

Dylan couldn't believe he was actually intrigued by his brother's suggestion. "Thanks, I appreciate the offer. Let's see how I do when I go back."

Wyatt nodded as if satisfied with the answer. "That's good enough for the time being. Now, I better get you home before Brenna sends out a search party."

Dylan arrived back at the cottage about nine o'clock. He'd enjoyed spending time with his brother, but knew that he had to get to his weight bench. Brenna should be up by now, but just in case, he was quiet when he came though the door.

The living room and kitchen were both empty. He headed for his room, noticing that Brenna's bedroom door was open, but she wasn't inside. That's when he heard the strange sound coming from the bathroom. He went closer and listened to the retching. After about ten seconds it happened again. Dylan decided that Brenna had to be pretty sick.

"Hey, Bren, you all right?"

Her answer came in a moan.

"Bren, I'm coming in," he warned, then opened the door to find her lying on the rug next to the tub. Still dressed in her pajamas, she had one hand across her stomach, the other across her eyes.

He managed to sit down on the lip of the tub. ''Are you all right?'' he repeated.

She groaned. ''Please, just leave and let me die in peace.''

''You feel that bad, then I'm calling Wyatt and we're taking you to the doctor.'' He braced his hand on the sink and started to stand, when she reached for him. The motion was too much and she lay back down.

''I'll be fine,'' she whispered.

''Like hell you will.'' Not knowing what else to do, Dylan took a damp washcloth, then leaned down and placed it over her face. He didn't like her ashen look.

Using his crutch, he went to her room and pulled the blanket off the end of the bed. He started back when he spotted the box of soda crackers on the nightstand. Soda crackers...vomiting... Suddenly he remembered the time a few days ago when he'd teased Brenna about knowing someone who was pregnant. She had looked so panicked over the discovery. It was beginning to add up.

Grabbing a stack of saltines, Dylan returned to the bathroom. He stood in the doorway and studied Brenna's slender body lying on the beige-tiled floor. Automatically his gaze was drawn to the slight curve of her stomach. A baby. The realization made him feel as if he'd been sucker punched in the gut.

He sat down on the tub's edge and covered her with the blanket, then made a towel into a pillow. He leaned down and offered her a cracker. ''Here, this might help, too.''

They exchanged a look that confirmed what he already suspected. ''Thank you.'' She took a small nibble, then another.

"How far along are you?" he asked with a flicker of hope that she would deny it.

She didn't even flinch. "Three and a half months."

"So you knew you were pregnant before you took this job."

She bit off another section of cracker. "Yes."

"I take it Jason is the baby's father." It hurt to state the fact, knowing that Brenna cared deeply for someone.

A lone tear ran down the side of her face. "Yes."

"Oh, God, you've been practically carrying me. Dammit, Brenna, you should never have taken this job."

This time she glared at him. "It was because of the baby that I had to. I need to be able to support my child, Dylan. And I've been doing my job."

"That's not the point," he argued. "You've been doing hard physical work. What about your parents? I should call them."

She grabbed his arm. "No, you can't. I haven't told them yet."

"Why the hell not? Surely they would help you with the baby."

"My parents have enough to deal with. They went into debt to help put me through college. I can't ask them for any more." She reached out and gripped his arm. "Please, Dylan, you can't call them."

He couldn't stand to see her upset. "Okay, okay, but you can't keep this a secret forever. Pretty soon they'll discover they're going to be grandparents just by looking at you." He was still having trouble handling the news himself.

"I will, but I need a little more time." Another tear fell. "If you want to fire me, I'll understand—"

"Stop talking crazy." Did she really think he was

such a cold bastard? "Besides, you promised to get me back on my feet."

She looked up at him with those golden-brown eyes. "Thank you."

Unable to resist, Dylan slid off the tub and down onto the floor beside her. He pulled her into his arms and cradled her head against his chest. Brenna didn't resist as his hands moved over her back, trying to soothe her fears.

"Did Jason know about the baby?"

"No," she began, her voice soft. "He died just a week after...I got pregnant."

A strange feeling of protectiveness came over him. "So you've been carrying this burden on your own?"

Brenna pulled away. "This baby isn't a burden. I love her." She was fierce as a lioness protecting her cub.

He refused to let her go and drew her back into his arms. "C'mon, darlin'. You can't act tough all the time. Let me help you," he whispered against her silky hair. "Together, we'll figure out something. I promise, you and the baby are going to be fine."

An hour later, after a warm shower, Brenna managed to pull herself together. She couldn't put it off any longer, she had to face him. In the kitchen, she found Dylan at the stove, stirring soup in a pan.

He turned to look at her. "Go sit down. You need something in your stomach." He poured the soup into a bowl and with the aid of his crutch, he carried it to the table.

Brenna didn't budge as she noticed how well he was moving around. "Hey, look at you." She pointed down at his leg.

"Oh, yeah, I've been testing putting a little weight on it this morning."

"How does it feel?"

"Not bad."

"Just don't overdo. If your leg starts hurting, get off it."

"Yes, ma'am. Now, I'm going to boss you around for a change. Sit down and eat. That kid of yours has to be starving."

"You don't need to take care of me, Dylan," she insisted. "I'm pregnant, not helpless. I got sick this morning because I ate too much at the party last night. I've been feeling pretty good lately."

He didn't look convinced. "You still need to eat. Sit."

He wasn't listening to her. "Okay, I'll let you do this, but let's not make a habit of it," she said and took a place at the table.

The last thing she wanted was to start relying on this man. She'd only end up getting hurt again. No, first she had to find out her fate. Did she still have a job?

"Dylan, now that you've had time to think about it, I need to know if you truly want me to stay." She began to eat her soup, the chicken broth surprisingly good.

Dylan sat down across from her. "Why wouldn't I? Like you said, you haven't slacked off in any of your duties, but I'll tell you right now, there's no heavy lifting. If I start to fall, let me fall."

"Anyone ever tell you that you're bossy?"

"Nope." He wiggled his eyebrows. "Sexy, maybe."

No doubt about that, Brenna thought as she broke out laughing. "Whoa, it's getting pretty crowded around here. I'm not sure there's enough room for you, me and your ego."

He started to answer, when a knock sounded on the

door. Suddenly feeling a whole lot better, Brenna got up to answer it. She had one problem resolved; she had her job for a while longer. She pulled open the door only to find Sean and Maggie Farren standing on the porch.

Another problem had just popped up. "Mom! Dad! What are you doing here?"

"Well, we're happy to see you, too," her mother said as she gave her daughter a hug.

Her father did the same. "Aren't you going to invite us in?"

"Oh, sure." Brenna stood aside trying to calm her racing heart. "I was just surprised to see you."

Petite Maggie Farren was forty-eight years old. She was a beautiful woman with amber eyes and brown hair. Her slender build was covered by a pair of jeans and a blouse. She looked around and her gaze stopped at Dylan. "Actually, we were over at the Circle B and Hank suggested we stop by. He said Mr. Gentry wouldn't mind."

"But Mom, I'm working right now."

Dylan got up from the table, leaning on it briefly for support. "It's all right, Brenna. Of course you can visit with your parents." He reached for his crutch and made his way across the room. "Hello, Mr. and Mrs. Farren. I'm Dylan, not Mr. Gentry. It's nice to finally meet you."

"It's nice to meet you, too," Maggie said, then sent an approving glance toward Brenna.

"Same here, son," her father said. "Call me Sean and she's Maggie," he answered as he shook Dylan's hand. Her father was a tall, slender man. All energy and muscle, with an easy smile and quick wit. "We've been pretty worried about you. Glad to see you're on the mend." He grinned and his blue eyes crinkled. "Of course, I bet my Brenna had something to do with it."

Dylan nodded. "She was a big part of it. She refused to let me give up. I owe her a lot."

"Brenna has always been strong-willed," Sean said. "I think that's because she has three brothers."

"I have no doubt she can handle herself just fine." Dylan looked at Brenna. "I'm going to take a shower. You stay here and visit with your parents as long as you want."

Brenna tried to keep the panic out of her voice, but it wasn't easy as she watched Dylan desert her. She turned to her parents. "I was planning on coming home this weekend."

Her mother frowned. "Brenna, are you feeling okay? You look a little pale." Maggie Farren's eyes were the same color as her own, and right now they were searching for answers.

Self-consciously, Brenna fiddled with the front of her sweatshirt. "How would you like some coffee, Mom?" She went to the kitchen, and her mother followed.

"Are you sure you're getting enough sleep?"

She busied herself scooping coffee into the coffee-maker. "Yes, I'm sleeping fine."

Maggie didn't take her gaze off her daughter and Brenna knew she wasn't fooling her mother. "Sean," Maggie called to her husband. "Would you go to the car and bring in the muffins that I baked?"

Her father left them alone. Once he was out the door, Maggie placed her hands on Brenna's shoulders. "Okay, missy, tell me the truth."

"Mom, there isn't anything…"

Her mother's gaze once again traveled over her daughter, then suddenly stopped at her slightly thicker waistline. She gasped as her trembling hand touched the growing curve. "You're pregnant."

Brenna felt light-headed as her mother gripped her by the arms. She'd never been able to lie, and what was the use? Everyone would know sooner or later. She nodded. "I'm sorry." She collapsed into her mother's arms. "I'm sorry," she cried.

Maggie's eyes filled, then she hugged her tightly. "Ssh, don't cry. Everything will be okay."

"I never meant for this to happen."

"I know." Maggie held on tighter. "But you've been blessed with a precious gift." When she finally released her daughter, she asked, "What are you planning to do?"

"Work, and support myself and the baby."

"And what about the child's father? Is he going to be involved in your lives?"

Before Brenna could tell her mother about Jason, her father came into the cottage carrying a basket of muffins. Immediately, he saw their tears. "What's the matter?"

Telling her father would be a lot harder for Brenna, but she had to do it. Her mother took her hand in a show of support. "Tell him, Brenna."

"I'm…going to have a baby, Dad."

Her father's eyes widened in surprise. "Oh, Bren…" After a second or two he frowned. "Are you okay?" He walked to her and drew her into his arms.

Brenna nodded against his chest. "Yes, I'm fine. The baby's fine."

He pulled back. "Good. Then you tell me who is responsible for this. He should do right by you."

"Dad, you don't understand—"

"I understand that the man has a responsibility to you and his child. Now, who is the father?"

Brenna didn't know how to tell him that the father was dead, that their first grandchild was going to be born out of wedlock.

She opened her mouth to speak, when she heard Dylan come into the room.

"That would be me, sir," he announced. "I'm responsible."

Brenna gasped at the lie, but was too stunned to speak.

Sean Farren walked to Dylan. Seconds ticked away as both men eyed one another. Then her father spoke. "If this is true, I expect you to do right by my daughter. And soon."

Chapter Six

"Are you crazy?" Brenna asked as she sank against the closed cottage door. The Farrens had just left for home.

Dylan wondered the same thing himself, but at the time it had seemed like the right thing to do. When he'd come out of the bedroom and heard Brenna's father grilling her, his protective instincts kicked in and he'd stepped forward.

"Probably, but it wouldn't be the first time."

She groaned and began to pace the room. "Now I have to go and tell my parents the truth." She started toward the kitchen then suddenly swung around to face him. "Didn't you realize that they would expect you to take care of us—to marry me?" She waved her hand as tears filled her eyes. "I'm sorry. I know you were trying to help me."

Dylan couldn't stand it any longer and he went to her. "Bren, don't cry. I'm the one who's sorry. I didn't mean to make things worse."

Somehow in the past weeks he'd come to care so much for Brenna, and it broke his heart to see her like this. He reached for her and she resisted momentarily, then crumbled into his arms, sobbing against his chest. For the first time, he realized how fragile she was. Brenna Farren wasn't weak by any stretch of the imagination, and no doubt she could handle this situation alone, but no way was he going to let her. There was a baby to think about. An innocent child who didn't deserve to start out this way.

"Bren...just listen to me for a minute." He continued to hold her, not wanting her to break the intimate contact. "I have an idea that might work. I want to go with you to talk to your parents." He shifted his weight on the crutch as his arm tightened around her back. "I want to assure them they don't have to worry about their daughter and grandchild...because we're getting married."

This time he couldn't hold on to her. Brenna jerked back. She swiped at her tears and glared at him. "This isn't funny, Dylan. And I don't appreciate the joke." She started to walk away, when he reached for her again.

"I'm not joking, Bren, and if you'll just listen to me—"

"Why should I, Dylan? I can't play this game. This isn't just my life we're talking about...it's my baby's, too."

He knew that all too well. "It's the child I'm thinking about. I know firsthand what it's like growing up with a father who doesn't want to claim his child. I know if Jason had lived things might have been different, but either way, it's not your baby's fault." He raised an eyebrow. "I take it your parents never knew about Jason."

Brenna shook her head, recalling the excuse she'd made to her mom and dad because Jason never showed on her graduation day. Later, she'd learned that he'd let her down to go canoeing on the Colorado River. "They were supposed to meet at my graduation, but he wasn't there. I told them we'd broken up."

"So they won't suspect that there had been another man in your life. I could be the little one's daddy."

"No! Everyone will know when the baby's born. Dylan, I'm over three months pregnant. I've only been here six weeks. Even if we were together the first night…" Her face flushed, realizing what she'd implied.

"Hey, I've been known to sweep women off their feet." He tossed her a sexy grin and more heat rose to her face.

Brenna realized that wouldn't be hard to believe. "But that's not me," she stressed. "I'm not like you. I'm not as casual about sex. I've only been with one man."

His smile faded. "Unlike me who's been with hundreds of women. Damn, it's a wonder how I ever had the time and energy to become a world-champion bull rider."

Brenna knew she'd hurt him. "I didn't mean it like that."

"Yes, you did," he said. "It might surprise you to know that bull riders are athletes. And with all the competition out there, you have to train and work out constantly. And even then you can get injured. On good days you still have trouble just getting out of bed, let alone partying all night." He raised a hand. "I'm not saying that I haven't shared some time with women, but they've all known I wasn't about to settle down. My focus has always been bull riding."

"All the more reason for you to forget this crazy idea."

"I disagree. If we're married, I don't have to worry about distractions on the circuit."

This was insane, she was actually thinking about it. Was she losing her mind? "What about the time difference as to when we met?"

He shrugged. "We can tell your parents that we met last summer at a rodeo."

"I can't lie to them."

"Bren, you haven't been honest with them as it is, or you would have told them about Jason and the baby when you first came home."

She blinked back the tears. Her mom and dad had already done so much for her. "I can't put this on them. They'll want to help, and also the ranch has been a big strain financially the past few years. I can't add to it."

"Then let me help you." He raised a soothing hand. "And think about your baby before you decide. I'm not suggesting a real marriage here. I know that's not what you need or want. This is so your parents will have the reassurance that you and their grandchild will be taken care of."

"I can take care of us," she insisted.

"Okay, so you don't need me financially," he conceded. "But what about taking my name? Unless you have something against it. I mean…because of Jack Randell."

She was shocked that he could think such a thing. "I thought you knew me better than that. Of course not. But you can't want to be saddled with a wife and child."

"Look, Bren. Unlike Wyatt, I never planned to marry…ever. I'm too much like my old man. But like I said before, being married has its advantages."

She bet it did, Brenna thought. Dylan "The Devil" Gentry could use his wedding ring to keep women from getting too attached to him. As she had.

"The real reason I want to do this is because of you." Those silvery-blue eyes bore into hers. His hand touched her cheek. "It was you who made me want to get up and walk. If I make it back on the circuit, it's because of you. Because you wouldn't give up on me, even when I wanted to give up on myself."

She shook her head. "You wanted to walk, Dylan, or you never would have worked so hard to get this far."

He hugged her. "Oh, Bren, let me help you now. You and the baby can live here in the cottage. I plan to be traveling the circuit. When I'm home, we can keep the same arrangement we've always had these past weeks."

Brenna was in big trouble. She was seriously considering his proposal.

"You can continue to work, or go back to school and maybe you can get your master's. In a few years when I retire, Wyatt has invited me to open a bull-riding school here at the Rocking R."

Brenna walked across the room. Being so close to him made it difficult to think. "With all these long-range plans, you forgot one thing, Dylan. What about the baby? He or she will get attached to you and then one day you'll walk away."

He looked as if she'd struck him. "I wouldn't do that, Bren. If we get married, I will always be there for the child."

Brenna realized that she wanted him to be there for *her,* too. Deep inside she knew this was a bad idea. Dylan was the type of man who loved danger and would never settle down. Could she handle him walking in and out of her life? Probably not.

"If we decide to go through with this, I think there should be a timetable. That way we both have an out, if we happen to find someone else. If we agree on this from the start, then no one gets hurt?"

"How much time?" he asked.

Once again, nothing seemed to deter him. "Say, six months after the baby is born. Then we should talk about continuing on…or ending it. We could let people think things didn't work because of your profession."

"If that's what you want," he said. "There's one more thing, Bren. I want as few people as possible to know the circumstances. As far as I'm concerned, this baby is mine. That means the kid thinks of me as his father. No matter what happens between us, I will always take care of the baby. Do you have a problem with that?"

His promise brought more tears to her eyes. She shook her head. "No. I don't have a problem."

Dylan smiled at her and something tightened around her heart. "Good." He limped across the room to her, leaned down and brushed his mouth across hers. She sucked in a breath, then all too soon, he pulled away.

"Now, I think we'd better go talk to your father before he comes back here with a rifle."

The next morning, Dylan got up before dawn. He finished his workout in record time, then Brenna supervised his therapy as if nothing between them had changed, despite the fact that a whole lot was about to.

But yesterday had changed everything else between them. That afternoon, they'd gone to visit the Farren Ranch and talked with Brenna's family, including her younger brothers Michael, James and Connor.

Surprisingly, Dylan found he had hated to fabricate

the details of their first meeting and their so-called relationship. It was Maggie Farren who had the most questions and reservations. None of that seemed to matter to
Sean Farren, not when Dylan told him their plans to
marry. Since the Catholic church had a six-month waiting period, the couple had no choice but to opt for a
civil ceremony. Arrangements would be made when he
and Brenna went into town later that day for the license.

After a quick shower and some breakfast, Dylan
headed down to the barn to tell his brother the news. He
found Wyatt with his champion bucking horse, Rock-a-
Billy, in the corral. The animal had hurt his leg in the
last rodeo and had been sent home to heal.

Dylan pulled the golf cart up beside the fence, got out
and grabbed his crutch. "How's it going?" he called to
his brother.

"Pretty good," Wyatt said as he walked out of the
corral. "The vet said Billy should be able to travel again
by next week."

"That's good news," Dylan answered. "Speaking of
news, I've got some. Brenna and I are getting married."

Except for the sound of Billy's restless whinny, there
was only silence. Finally Wyatt looked at him. "How
long has this been going on?"

"Long enough," Dylan said, not knowing what else
to say but feeling he owed his brother the truth. "And
another thing, Brenna is pregnant."

That got Wyatt's attention. "That's some therapy."
He stopped. "There's more, isn't there?"

Dylan shrugged. "It's not anybody's business."

"I hope you don't bunch me into that category? I'm
your brother. Now, tell me the rest of the story."

Wyatt had always been overprotective, and the last
thing Dylan wanted was for his big brother to try to talk

him out of this marriage. "This isn't for anyone else, but Brenna was pregnant when you hired her. The baby's father was killed in a hang-gliding accident three months ago. When her parents learned about the pregnancy two days ago, I more or less told them I was the father."

Wyatt made a whistling sound, then surprised him when he smiled. "You still dive in with both feet, don't you?"

"When I have to," Dylan admitted. "Look, bro, it was Bren who helped get me back on my feet. I couldn't let her handle this situation alone."

"So you offered to marry her and raise her child."

"Yeah. It doesn't change my plans, though. I still plan to ride again. But that baby needs a father. So they'll be staying on in the cottage, if that's okay."

"As far as I'm concerned, that's your place for as long as you want it."

"Thanks. If the doctor okays me to ride, I want the Rocking R to be my home base. I want to come here in between rodeos."

"I'm liking the sound of this," Wyatt said, grinning.

"I've also been thinking about that bull-riding school you mentioned. Maybe in the future we can talk about it some more. Sounds like something I might like to do."

"That sounds real good." Wyatt lifted his cowboy hat and reset it on his head. "Funny how a woman can get you to look at things…differently."

"I'm not changing my goal," Dylan protested. "It's still to get back on a bull. But a man needs to think about investing in his future."

He had plenty of money in the bank, but it wouldn't last forever if he didn't make plans. He should start a college fund for the baby, and if Brenna wanted to go back to school.

"When is this wedding taking place?" Wyatt asked.

"Brenna and I are going today to make the arrangements. Probably next week sometime. Will you be my best man?"

"I'd be happy to."

Wyatt put his arm across Dylan's shoulders. "Looks like the last of the brothers is about to get hitched. I guess when we find the right woman, we don't waste any time."

"This isn't like that," Dylan insisted.

"Yeah, that's what we all said."

She didn't remember saying yes.

Now, two days later, Brenna stood in front of a three-way mirror in a local bridal shop, admiring the ivory, tea-length dress she was going to wear when she married Dylan.

The fitted, off-the-shoulder bodice had a scalloped neckline and long sleeves that ended in points at her wrists. The skirt was gathered at her waist and draped softly around her. Brenna touched her slightly rounded stomach, trying to calm the butterflies.

"Oh, Brenna, you look beautiful," her mother cried. She grasped her hands together, gazing lovingly at her daughter. "And your grandmother's pearls will be perfect. Simple, yet elegant."

Brenna wanted to call a halt to this madness. It was all going too fast for her. How did things get so out of control? That she knew. When she and Dylan had gone to her parents' house, everyone just took for granted that they'd be married. In fact, her brothers had played her protectors, practically threatening Dylan if he didn't do his duty.

She didn't want to be anyone's duty.

Now she was marrying a man she barely knew. A man who wasn't good husband and father material. A man who would never give up his dangerous profession for her.

"I think this dress is beautiful," Maggie Farren said. "Although the dress with the antique lace was also pretty. What do you think?"

Brenna didn't want to think. She wanted to run away, but she couldn't. There was her baby to think of. A baby she already loved, and couldn't wait to hold in her arms. And as much as she wanted to handle her life on her own, she couldn't deny her child two parents. She glanced at her mother's glowing face. She knew she couldn't burden her parents again. There was only one way, and that was to accept Dylan's generous offer.

The salesclerk walked up. "You look absolutely breathtaking," she said. "That dress is made for you."

Brenna glanced at the price tag and gasped. There was no way she or her parents could afford to pay this amount. "Is there something a little more...reasonable?"

The salesclerk smiled. "You don't have to worry about the cost. Mr. Gentry left instructions with us to let you pick any dress you want. That price wasn't a problem."

"But I can't..." Brenna hesitated and looked at her mother.

"I think we'll take this one," Maggie said. "And we'll need shoes and undergarments." With a nod, the saleswoman walked away.

"Mom!" Brenna gasped. "What are you doing?"

"The man loves you. If he wants you to have a beautiful dress, then let him buy it for you."

"But you don't understand…"

"I understand more than you think. There is nothing wrong with letting your future husband give you a nice wedding." She blinked back sudden tears. "I'm sorry that your father and I can't."

"Oh, Mom, I didn't exactly give you any time to plan one." They both laughed.

"We're getting a double bonus. A grandchild."

Brenna was becoming excited. "So you're happy?"

"I'm so happy that you've found a man who obviously loves you."

Brenna had to fight her own tears. Her mother was so wrong. She was marrying a man she barely knew, but worse, one she was quickly falling in love with. Someone who could never return that love.

That alone could be disastrous.

Six days later, with the aid of his cane, Dylan stepped off the elevator followed by Wyatt, Maura and the kids. He wore a new navy suit, a crisp white shirt and a blue silk tie that felt as if it was strangling him inch by inch. He'd even had his hair trimmed, and when Brenna came into view, he knew all the hassle was worth it. She stole his breath away.

Today, she was all soft and feminine…and beautiful in her ivory dress. He felt a sudden stirring and had to shake away the feeling. Gripping a florist box, he started toward her.

Brenna looked up as he approached. Her auburn hair was pulled up on her head with tiny flowers tucked into the curls. Her golden-brown eyes were wide and fearful as a skittish filly.

"Bren…" He stopped in front of her. "You're beautiful."

She released a breath. "Thank you. You look handsome."

He noticed the crowd of people growing, then took hold of her hand and nodded behind him. "You think we can go over there so I can talk to you?"

If possible, she looked more nervous than he did. Together they started off toward a little alcove at the end of the hall.

"You're doing real well with the cane," she remarked. "Just remember not to overdo."

"Stop playing therapist, Brenna," he said. "I feel fine."

"Sorry, it's a habit." Her gaze finally met his. "Look, Dylan, if you decided not to go through with the ceremony, I'll understand. I mean, it was a crazy idea."

Dylan's finger covered her lips to quiet her. "I'm not changing my mind, Bren. I brought you over here so I can give you this." He leaned his cane against the wall, then opened the box revealing a bridal bouquet of ivory roses and orchids, trimmed in lavender and surrounded with greenery and white ribbon.

"Oh, Dylan. It's beautiful." Her hands trembled as she lifted the flowers from the box. "Thank you."

"You need to thank Maura. She put the bouquet together. She told me what each flower means, but I forget, so you'll have to ask her."

Brenna could hardly believe Dylan's sweet gesture. "I will when I thank her." The elevator chimed and more of the Randells stepped off. "This is turning out to be a little bigger than I expected."

Dylan glanced toward the crowd. "Once I told Maura, things got out of control."

It was all so overwhelming. "There's still time to back out," she said.

"How can I convince you I don't want to back out?" He smiled. "Maybe there is a way." He took her by the arm and drew her close. Dylan's gaze locked on hers just as he lowered his head, then his mouth touched hers, gently. Slowly the kiss deepened as his arm came around her, drawing her against him. The contact drove every rational thought from her head and she grabbed hold of his jacket to keep from sliding to the floor. Finally, hearing someone calling to them, they broke apart.

They looked around to find Wyatt. "It's time," he said.

"Good." With a wink, Dylan retrieved his cane, then took her hand, and they headed to the judge's chambers.

Somehow everyone managed to crowd into the room. "Seems these family weddings are becoming a habit," Hank Barrett said. "This makes number six in the past few years."

Dylan took Brenna's hand as the judge directed them to stand in the front of the room. Beside the groom was Wyatt, and next to the bride was her matron of honor, Maura. Her parents stood behind them along with her brothers.

Brenna took a long breath and released it as Judge Clark began with, "Dearly beloved…"

During the ceremony she kept her attention on Dylan. Finally she heard, "You may kiss your bride."

When Dylan turned to her, she thought she was prepared for his kiss. Then his mouth captured hers and she was swept away once again. All she could do was put her arms around his neck and hold on. Finally her new husband pulled back and winked at her. Before she could say a word, they were being pulled apart with offers of congratulations.

They were swept away to sign the wedding certificate, then Wyatt invited everyone back to the Rocking R where Maura, and the rest of the Randell wives, had planned a reception for the happy couple. Brenna wasn't sure she could carry this off. Then she looked at her mother's face and saw how happy she was. She knew she had to keep playing the game.

It was too late to turn back now.

The wedding guests broke out in cheers as Dylan walked his new wife into Wyatt and Maura's house. He was a little taken aback by all the attention they were getting over this simple ceremony.

Dylan glanced at Brenna and saw her smile and he was glad that he'd let Maura go all out for this day. He was a little surprised by how much he'd been enjoying himself, especially kissing his new wife. Things might change when they were alone, so he was going to take advantage of all the opportunities. Like now. He pulled her close and pressed his lips against Brenna's and the crowd cheered once again.

"I'll get even with you, Gentry," Brenna threatened with a smile. "Your therapy is going to double."

His mouth captured hers once again, causing her to swallow the rest of her words. Brenna forgot her thoughts, forgot even to breathe. This had to stop. She pulled back. "Aren't you overdoing it a little?"

He grinned. "We want to convince everyone, don't we?"

"I think getting married is convincing enough," she said as her mother came up to her.

"Oh, Brenna, you were beautiful." She had tears in

her eyes. "I know it wasn't the church wedding we wanted for you, but the ceremony was lovely just the same. You two look so happy."

Dylan hugged Maggie. "I'm going to do everything possible to keep your girl happy."

"I know you will, Dylan." The older woman smiled, then walked off to greet other guests.

"You're making an awful lot of promises," Brenna said.

"And I'm going to keep them. Can't you stop worrying for just a little while?" He pulled her close. "It's going to be okay, Bren. Trust me." He kissed the end of her nose. "Will you?"

She knew she was crazy but she nodded anyway.

"Good. Come on. I believe there's a cake with our name on it waiting for us in the dining room."

He took her into the next room where they posed for pictures before cutting the cake, then they went around and visited with everyone, thanking them for coming and for all the gifts.

Wyatt then quieted the crowd as he stood next to Maura, both holding a champagne glass.

"To my brother and his bride. Dylan, I never thought there would be a woman who could put up with you, let alone make you want to settle down. Brenna, welcome to the family. May your life together be filled with happiness, joy and most importantly, love." He raised his glass. "To Dylan and Brenna."

Next, Chance Randell took the stage. "Since I'm the oldest, I'm speaking for my family." He turned to the bride and groom. "Dylan and Brenna, we would like to welcome you as neighbors. We hope we to get the opportunity to get to know you both better. We got together and thought the best wedding gift we could give you is a honeymoon.'' He reached into his pocket and pulled out a key. ''The family would like to give you the bridal cabin in Mustang Valley. It's stocked with food and enough wood to last you at least a week.'' He grinned. ''The best part is that the guest ranch is closed for the season, so you'll be totally alone.''

Brenna could barely swallow, but she somehow managed to thank Chance and the brothers for the wonderful gesture. Soon after, the party broke up and everyone headed home. Brenna offered to help Maura clean up.

Her new sister-in-law smiled. ''You can't, you and your husband will be leaving soon.''

Brenna wasn't planning on going anywhere near the honeymoon cabin. ''We can go later,'' she said.

''No need. We've taken care of everything.'' Just then Wyatt came in, pulling a suitcase for Brenna and a duffel bag for Dylan. ''Your mother packed your clothes, Brenna. Now you two have no excuses. Just follow Wyatt to his truck and he'll drive you to your honeymoon destination.''

Brenna's pulse pounded. She hadn't planned on going anywhere. She looked at Dylan.

''Then I guess we're ready,'' her new husband said. ''Come on, honey, it looks like they're trying to get rid of us.'' With cheers from the Randell family, he took her hand and walked her outside to the truck.

There was definitely no turning back now.

Chapter Seven

Twenty minutes later, Wyatt let the newlyweds off at the narrow dirt road that led to the cabins. Since there were no vehicles allowed in Mustang Valley they had to use a golf cart for the three-minute drive to the isolated cabin.

"Looks like we're here," Dylan announced as he pulled up to the one-story split-log structure. He climbed out and retrieved their bags. Brenna didn't move as she looked around the secluded area. About a hundred yards away there was a rocky-bottom creek. Although most of the trees were bare, the view of the valley was still spectacular. A feeling of serenity washed over her as she turned toward the lone cabin surrounded by shrubs and trees.

This was a perfect place for a couple who didn't want to be disturbed.

She got out and came around to help, feeling a little of the calm leaving her just in time to see another cart heading away over the rise. Someone had probably come here to check out the cabin. She took her suitcase from Dylan so he could handle his cane. He made his way to the small porch and used his key to unlock the door. Suddenly when he held out his hand to her, all of today's events hit Brenna. She'd married this man. For real— but not real. Now she was on a not-for-real honeymoon. Great.

With a tight grip on her suitcase handle, she walked across the threshold, but nothing could have prepared her for what she found inside. The main room was aglow with dozens of candles and a fire in the hearth. Two love seats were across from each other; in between sat an old steamer trunk. There was a small kitchen area and a round table with two place settings of china and a centerpiece vase of white roses and candles. In the alcove sat a huge four-poster bed, draped in a wine-colored satin comforter adorned with dozens of pillows, and rose petals scattered about. More candles and flowers lined the area.

This would be anyone's dream honeymoon, but not hers. She turned to Dylan. "Okay, what now?" she asked.

He sank against the door. "Believe me, this place gives me plenty of ideas, but I don't think you want to know what they are."

No, she didn't. "How long are we expected to stay here?" She eyed the king-size bed. *One* bed. The only other place to sleep was on one of the short sofas.

"I don't think it's safe to show our faces for at least a few days."

Dylan was going to kill Wyatt. He knew that his brother had a lot to do with this setup. In other circumstances he wouldn't mind spending the weekend with a beautiful woman, but this wasn't a good idea. Not if he was going to keep his hands off her.

"Look, Brenna," he began. "I had no idea they were planning to give us the cabin. If I had, I'd have made some excuse for us not to come here."

"Dylan, it's all right," she assured him. "It's not as if we haven't been living together the past six weeks. We can handle the next few days."

Sure he could, he told himself. "Okay. Why don't you take the bed. I'll sleep on the sofa."

"You can't possibly fit," she argued. "I'll sleep there."

"No way. You take the bed," he insisted.

"But your leg will cramp up."

He shifted his weight onto his good leg. "You and the baby need room too, and sleep."

"I'm not that big…yet. Besides, the baby is comfortable and we get plenty of sleep."

"Any suggestions?"

He eyed the huge bed. "We can…share the bed," he said.

"What?" She looked startled.

"Why not, it's big enough," he reasoned. "We can put pillows down the middle of the mattress so neither of us will…infringe on the other's space. I'll even sleep on top of the covers. We won't even know we're in the same bed." Right. Who was he kidding? He'd been so aware of Brenna that he hadn't been able to think rationally since that first kiss.

She looked unconvinced and tired.

"Are you feeling okay?"

"Just a little tired…and hungry."

He smiled. "How about some supper?"

She nodded. "That sounds good. I was too nervous to eat at the reception."

"We had cake." How could he forget feeding her, then kissing her, tasting the sugary frosting off her lips. He went to the refrigerator and opened it, hoping the frigid air would cool his jets. "Oh, man. Will you look at all this food?"

Brenna came up beside him to see several casseroles and salads crowding the shelves, plus a big platter of fried chicken. There were cheeses and olives, a cheesecake and two pies, some wine and fruit juices.

"Looks like the family has been busy," Brenna said. "This must have been what that person was doing here."

Being stuck here might not be so bad, he thought. "What would you like for your wedding supper, Mrs. Gentry?"

Her brown-eyed gaze shot to him. "Anything is fine."

Dylan saw her nervousness and closed the door. "Brenna, you have to stop looking at me like I'm a stranger trying to have my way with you."

"But…we were married today."

He grinned. "I know, I was there."

"And so was my family," she said. "They think this marriage is for real."

"It's as real as you want to make it," he said, leaning on his cane. His leg was beginning to ache from standing so long. Brenna noticed his discomfort, too.

"You should be off your feet." She urged him toward the table.

Dylan didn't argue as he collapsed into a chair. "I guess I overdid it a little today," he said as she began massaging his leg. It felt heavenly, maybe too much so.

"That's enough," he told her, stopping her hands. "I'll be fine if I'm off it for a while. After I fix us supper."

She started to argue about that.

"You need to relax, too," he insisted.

"I've been getting plenty of rest."

He shook his head. "You're not cooking tonight." He got to his feet. "Now, you sit and I'll call you when things are ready."

She opened her mouth, then closed it. "Fine. But I'm going to help you. Just let me change out of my dress and I'll be right back."

She started to walk away, when Dylan took hold of her hand. "If I haven't said it already, you looked beautiful today."

She flushed. "You mentioned it earlier, but it's nice to hear. Thank you. And thank you again for this dress and the flowers, though you spent too much money."

He shook his head. "Seeing you today made it worth every penny."

Dylan's grip on her hand tightened, and he fought everything inside him not to lower his head and capture her sweet mouth, to pull her soft body against him. He bit back a groan and finally released her.

Silently Brenna retrieved her suitcase and disappeared into the bathroom. He hissed out a long breath and made a beeline to the refrigerator, praying the cold and the sight of food would change the direction of his thoughts.

When Brenna returned ten minutes later, her hair was down and she was wearing jeans and a bright pink sweater. Dylan still had on his suit pants, but had removed his jacket and tie and rolled up his shirtsleeves.

They sat down at the small table in front of the window overlooking the valley. The sun had gone down, but soft moonlight silhouetted the large trees. They ate cold chicken, Caesar salad and some of the cheesecake.

Afterward, Dylan added logs to the fire and they sat on the sofa, talking about the day. The tension between them began to fade away but that only lasted until it was time for bed.

Once again, Brenna went into the bathroom to change. Dylan quickly undressed in the alcove, hanging up his suit and some clothes in the closet. He searched his bag, found a pair of pajama bottoms and silently thanked his brother. After one last check around the cabin, he secured the locks and checked the dying flame in the hearth. He still avoided the bed as he anxiously paced around, realizing he was actually nervous.

This was ridiculous. He hadn't been this edgy since he'd tried to cop a feel with Becky Phillips when he was sixteen. He wasn't a teenager anymore, and this wasn't a game. He'd married Brenna today to protect her and the baby, not to take advantage of the situation.

That didn't change the fact he wanted her...badly.

At least at the cottage they had their own rooms to go to for privacy. Here they were practically in each other's pocket. Worse, they were about to share the same bed— a honeymoon bed surrounded by soft candlelight and the sweet fragrance of flowers.

He went around and blew out candles, then turned on the lamp beside the bed and sat down on the mattress. He heard the bathroom door open. His breath caught as Brenna stepped out from the shadows.

"Sorry, this was all my mother packed for me."

She was wearing a champagne-colored gown. The straps were thin, exposing her delicate shoulders. The satin material draped over her full breasts, revealing the hard points of her nipples. His gaze raked over the slight swell of pregnancy, the curve of her hips until the fabric stopped midcalf, showing off her shapely legs. He swallowed. He was a dead man. There was no way he was going to survive this night.

Dylan was having the best dream ever. He opened his eyes to find sunlight shining through the cabin window and discovered he wasn't dreaming.

Brenna's soft, warm body was curled against his. A throaty moan escaped her mouth as her fingers skimmed over his chest. He sucked in a breath, trying not to respond to the wonderful torture. And she wasn't finished. She moved closer, rubbing herself against his already aroused body. Another moan.

His heart raced in his chest. He had to put a stop to this or he was going to explode—or die.

Reluctantly, he placed his hand on her arm. "Bren," he whispered, but she didn't open her eyes. He shook her a little harder. "Bren, wake up."

Her eyes still remained closed. She made another throaty sound and moved on top of him, her mouth inches from his. "Kiss me."

His heart nearly came out of his chest and his groin tightened painfully. This was more than any man could tolerate. He surrendered.

"If that's what you want." His arms wrapped around her and pulled her upward so his mouth could meet hers in a hungry kiss. He didn't hesitate and slipped his tongue past her lips and delved inside to sample her sweetness. She groaned again, pressing her body closer. Her satin gown only stimulated him more, heightening his pleasure.

Damn, she was pure temptation and he wanted her.

Bad. But not like this. He gripped her shoulders and pushed her back.

"Bren," he breathed. "Wake up!"

Finally her amber eyes blinked open. Another shot of need surged through him and he wished he had kept his mouth shut.

When Brenna realized where she was and what she was doing she scrambled off him. "Oh!"

She tried to move away, but he kept her from going too far. "Please don't go."

She hugged the blanket closer as she tried to calm herself. She couldn't look Dylan in the eye. "How did I end up on your side of the bed?"

"You were probably cold and seeking warmth."

Oh, sure. She was definitely warm. "I'm sorry."

He rolled to his side, resting his head on his hand. "I wasn't complaining, but I didn't want things to go any further when you weren't...aware of what was going on."

"Nothing is going on. I was asleep. I had no idea what I was doing."

He smiled. "There's nothing wrong with us wanting each other. In fact, it's natural."

She couldn't let that happen. In the end, he was going to leave her. She couldn't let another man hurt her, especially when it involved her child. "If you married me hoping to get someone to warm your bed then we better end this now."

"Just hold it right there," he said and climbed out of bed. "I can't deny I want you, but I don't take advantage of women." He went to his bag, pulled out some clothes, then limped to the bathroom, but paused before going in. "If you would stop lying to yourself, you'd realize that you want me as much as I want you. For your information, I wasn't the one who initiated the kiss this morning.'' He went into the bathroom and slammed the door.

Oh, God, Dylan was right. She'd been all over him. Her body was still tingling from the aftereffects. What had gotten into her? Better yet, what was she going to do now? How could they live together like this? She heard the shower go on. She closed her eyes and pictured a naked Dylan stepping into the stall. She didn't have to imagine much since she'd already seen him without clothes.

Pushing away those thoughts, she got out of bed intending to get dressed, then realized her suitcase was in the bathroom. Looking down at her revealing gown, she knew she had to put on something else. She went to the closet and found Dylan's white shirt and slipped it on. After buttoning it, she rolled the sleeves up as she walked into the kitchen.

First, she started the coffee, then took eggs and milk out of the refrigerator. After putting bacon in the microwave, she made up the mixture for French toast. Somehow she had to make amends to Dylan, and hoped that a hearty breakfast would help smooth things between them.

Dylan had handled this morning all wrong. He dipped his head under the showerhead. Now he had to figure out a way to bring things back to the way they were. He turned off the water and stepped out of the shower. Reaching for a towel, he knew he had to stay focused on his goal: to get back to bull riding. Brenna was helping him, and in return, he was helping her. He had to remember that.

He pulled on underwear, then his jeans and zipped

them up. He wiped the steam off the mirror and stood in front of one of the two sinks in the oversize bathroom. This place had been well thought out by the designer. There was a double shower stall. Off in the corner was a large Jacuzzi tub. No doubt meant for newlyweds' bathing needs. He pictured Brenna sitting in the deep tub, with watery bubbles dancing over her breasts. He groaned. Don't go there, he told himself as he ran the razor over his face.

She doesn't want any part of me. Not that way. He rinsed off the rest of the lather and realized he hadn't brought in a shirt. Great, she'll think he did it on purpose. He opened the door, glad to discover she wasn't in bed. He grabbed a shirt from the closet and put it on. Then, using his cane, he headed to the kitchen and the enticing smell of coffee.

When he turned at the counter, he stopped and so did his heart, then it began pumping like crazy at the sight of Brenna Farren Gentry dressed in his shirt. He took another breath, but it didn't help. She had the longest, smoothest and shapeliest legs he'd ever seen. He never had been interested in women's feet, but hers were…slender and delicate, each toe polished a rosy pink.

He shook his head. Oh, Lord. He was losing it.

Finally she swung around and blinked in surprise. "Oh, Dylan. I didn't hear you come out of the bathroom."

How could she not hear his heart drumming? "I just got here." He walked to the coffeemaker and poured himself some needed brew. After several sips of courage, he decided he had to face her. "Bren, about this morning—"

"No, Dylan, you were right," she said. "I made too

much out of it. Besides, I was the…guilty one. I was on your side of the bed.''

Hell, she was on top of him, but he wasn't going to bring that up. ''I still shouldn't have gotten so angry.'' He stepped closer. ''But believe me, Bren…I would never do anything you didn't want. Ever.''

Her amber gaze met his. ''I know. But you were also right about us being attracted to one another.'' Tears swam in her eyes. ''I don't want…''

It was natural to go to her and take her in his arms. ''Ssh, Bren. I swear, nothing will happen. If we make it through this…honeymoon, things will be easier back at the cottage.''

''What do we do?''

He didn't have a damn idea. He nodded toward the frying pan. ''How about some of that French toast?''

She laughed. ''I think *that* I can handle.'' She turned back to the stove.

Dylan went for his coffee, knowing the last thing he needed was more caffeine. He'd better concentrate on something else, like his therapy. Exhaust his body with exercise so he would stop having carnal thoughts about Brenna.

He doubted that he'd ever forget how she looked in his shirt.

Without regular exercise equipment, they had to improvise the therapy session. For a bench, Brenna directed Dylan to the trunk in front of the fireplace. Using a blanket to pad the table, she began the stretching exercises for his hamstrings, working her way to his thighs. They usually carried on a easy conversation during the routine, but not this morning.

"We'll go light today," she said. "But I don't want your leg to stiffen up."

"We can't let that happen," Dylan grunted, knowing that wasn't the part of his anatomy he was worried about.

He had never been so aware of Brenna's touch as she worked his damaged leg to regain more range of motion. Then came the resistance training as she used her body weight to press against his bent leg. After each series of reps, she massaged away any stiffness. The time went by agonizingly slow until finally they finished the session.

"I think we can stop for now." She stood over him. "But I want you to sit in the whirlpool for fifteen minutes."

"You never give up, do you?"

She raised an eyebrow, looking bossy and cute. "Do you want me to?"

"No." He wiped his face with the towel, then managed to get to his feet. He got his cane and followed her to the bathroom. She turned on the water and adjusted the temperature and jets.

Dylan had stripped off his shirt, standing next to the tub in his jeans. When Brenna stood, her gaze went to his chest, then moved upward. He couldn't miss the yearning in those whiskey-hued eyes. Damn, he was dying here.

"I don't think it's too hot," she said, changing the subject. "But you might want to test the water before you get in."

Dylan glanced down at the large tub. "You know, there's plenty of room. Want to join me?"

"No! No, thank you." Her voice was breathy.

"Come on, Bren...it's like a hot tub. And you worked

out just as hard as I did. Besides, who will know?'' he teased. ''I'll stay on the other side.''

She went to the cupboard. ''I'll be just in the next room if you need me.'' She took out a towel and put it on the counter. ''I don't have a swimsuit.'' She turned and walked out.

''Great! Now that's a picture that's going to help me relax. Brenna naked,'' Dylan grumbled as he stripped out of his sweats and climbed into the bubbling water. He lay his head against the back of the tub and closed his eyes and this morning flashed into his head. The feel of Brenna's body tucked against him. Her hands on him, wanting him. He groaned and sank under the water in frustration.

So far, marriage was hell.

That afternoon they ventured outside. The day was sunny and warm and perfect for a walk. Brenna was dressed in black stretch pants and a long, blue pullover sweater when she walked out of the cabin. She wanted to take the golf cart, but Dylan insisted that he could make it down to the creek on his own power. She didn't argue, figuring she could come back and get the cart if the walk turned out to be too much for him.

Brenna packed some food and her camera, hoping to get a glimpse of the mustangs. She found herself excited about the excursion. Over the years she'd heard about the ponies that roamed this valley.

Slowly, with Brenna keeping a constant eye on Dylan, she led the way down the rise and they began a lazy stroll along the rocky bank.

''Would you stop?'' he asked as he made his way over the uneven ground. ''I told you I could handle this.'' He stopped by the water. ''See, I'm still in one piece.''

She ignored his sarcasm. "Why don't we find a spot and sit a while. I could stand a break. We've walked a long way."

He grinned. "I know."

"Pretty proud of yourself, huh?"

"Wait until you see me toss away this cane."

She couldn't wait. But when that happened, he wouldn't need her any longer, either. "We'll have a party," she promised.

They came to a grove of trees and a clearing where she spread the blanket, then sat down and glanced around. If she looked closely she could make out the other cabins marking the edge of the valley, but the structures were not so noticeable that they disturbed the valley or the inhabitants. There was also Travis and Josie Randell's house tucked away in the hills over the other side, but several trees hid most of the structure from prying eyes. She sighed. It must be paradise to live here.

She looked up at Dylan. "You should sit down."

"Yes, Mother."

Okay, so she was being a little protective. She told herself it had nothing to do with the fact the man was now her husband. "That's 'Mother sir.'"

He laughed and sank to the blanket. He, too, seemed to be caught up in the valley's beauty. "Who'd ever think a place like this still existed?"

"It's so peaceful," she said. "No wonder the mustangs come here."

"Speaking of which, I think they're about to make an appearance."

Dylan scooted up behind her and pointed in the direction of a small group of horses that were walking their way. A white stallion led the group, followed by a buckskin mare and a foal scurrying to keep up. There were several others, a chestnut, a paint, all distinct in looks due to the mixture of Spanish ancestry and many other breeds.

"Oh, they're beautiful," Brenna breathed as she reached for her camera. Without moving from her spot she snapped several pictures of the animals. Finally the horses moved on.

"They don't seem to be bothered that we're here," she said, feeling Dylan shift closer to her. She knew she should move away, resist the temptation of starting something. "My dad said that Hank has protected them for years. As you can see it's as if they know that they won't be harmed by us."

"What happens when the herd gets too large?"

"Hank and the Randells round up some of them and hold an auction. Mustangs make good saddle horses."

"I know. My first horse was a little chestnut mare. I was eleven years old. It took me weeks to catch her, but I finally got her eating out of my hand."

Brenna didn't doubt that. There wasn't a female alive that could resist this man. She raised her camera and snapped another shot.

"That's a pretty nice camera you've got."

She held up her gift to herself. "I did splurge a little. There was a time I dreamed of being a professional photographer. I wanted to see the world and work for CNN or some other big news company."

"What changed your mind?"

"Reality hit. I needed to make a living and support myself. It would have taken years to get established."

"You can't give up on your dreams."

"I haven't. They've just changed. I'm doing what I love to do. And I can take fabulous baby pictures. Who's to say I can't be the next Anne Geddes?"

"I have no doubt you could be, whoever she is." His arms were around her, pulling her into an embrace, and she wasn't resisting. And she should be, especially when his mouth went to her ear and he whispered, "Your baby is lucky to have you as its mother."

A shiver went through her as his hand rested against her stomach. "I...I'm going to try to be the best mom possible."

"I want to help you," he said. "I want to be a part of the baby's life."

How many times had she heard similar promises? How many times had Jason disappointed her? During the four months they'd lived together, she had learned not to expect anything from him.

She turned toward Dylan. His silvery-blue eyes were mesmerizing, sending her heart racing. "Please, Dylan, you don't have to make me promises. We both know you'll be going back to the circuit." Her problem was, she wanted this man to come home to *her*.

"But I'll be coming back to the ranch."

"Dylan..."

He placed his finger against her mouth to stop her words. "Don't say anything."

Then he lowered his head and his lips touched hers. Any rational thought fled from Brenna's head as Dylan worked his magic.

Chapter Eight

Dylan wanted to keep touching Brenna, kissing her, tasting her, but he knew he had to let go of her. Reluctantly, he pulled away. When he raised his head and saw the desire in her eyes, he nearly changed his mind.

"Damn, you're a tempting woman." He placed another light kiss on her lips.

She blushed.

"There's a rider on horseback who just came over the rise," he said. "We should make sure he gets an eyeful and make this look real."

"I guess we should," she agreed, then surprised him as she moved forward and kissed him.

Dylan gripped her by the arms and turned her in his lap, giving him better access to her delicious mouth. When he heard her soft whimper, he broke off the kiss, before things got too far out of hand. Since someone was about to interrupt them, he needed to keep his head. He drew back and saw her stunned look.

"We'll continue this later," he whispered, seeing Hank Barrett ride up. "In private."

He turned toward Hank as the older man climbed off his mount. Dylan got to his feet and Brenna followed his lead. She straightened her hair and her clothes as the rancher made his way to them.

"Hank, good to see you," Brenna said.

Dylan offered his hand. "Hello, Hank. We can't thank you enough for letting us stay here. This place is wonderful."

"Glad you like it, but I doubt if you two are any more anxious to see me right now than I am to be here. I drew the short straw and I'm here to relay a message. The weather people are predicting a storm coming in tonight. I figured you wouldn't care, but I was sent to warn you so you can pack up and head home if you want. I told everyone that neither of you could care less about a little rain."

Dylan glanced up at the clear, blue sky. "When is the storm supposed to get here?"

"Around midnight, maybe earlier." He pulled a small cell phone out of his pocket. "Just in case things get bad, you can call and we'll come and get you out. All the family numbers are in the phone." He paused as he cocked an eyebrow. "Unless you want to leave now? Think about it." With a nod, Hank walked away, then climbed up on his horse and rode off.

"I guess we should go back to the cabin and call your brother to come and get us," Brenna said.

"Hold it just a minute," he said. "Do you really want to leave?"

She knew she should say yes, but after the kiss they'd shared she was having trouble thinking clearly. "It's probably for the best. I mean with the rain and all…what if we're stuck here?''

Dylan tossed her one of his drop-dead-sexy grins. ''Well, we don't have to worry about starving to death.''

We could get into so much trouble, she thought, unable to get the idea of sharing the whirlpool tub with him out of her head.

''Come on, Bren…let's stay. We have a right to relax and enjoy ourselves. We've both been working hard the past two months, especially you. And what about all that food in the cabin? We can't let it go to waste.'' He stepped closer, lowered his head, and his mouth touched hers, gently.

''What was that for?'' she asked.

''Just because you look so damn sexy.'' He took another nibble. ''Tell me if you want me to stop.''

''You don't play fair, Dylan Gentry. I'm in a weakened condition and you're taking advantage.''

''You're right. This could lead to a lot of trouble. Trouble that neither one of us is ready for.'' His expression was serious. ''I would like to stay the night, and I promise that I won't lay a hand on you. You're safe with me, Bren.''

Now *that* was just what every girl wanted to hear.

Around midnight, as predicted, lightning lit up the dark sky. Then came the thunder rumbling through the valley. It seemed to rattle the cabin. Brenna lay in bed wide awake, listening to the soft snores coming from Dylan's side. How could anyone sleep through all the noise?

Usually, Brenna wasn't afraid of storms. When you lived in Texas, thunderstorms were a fact of life. She just didn't care to be all alone during a severe storm.

This one promised to be a doozy. The wind whistled and rain pelted the windows. The building was sound, but that thought didn't comfort her at all.

All of a sudden Dylan turned to her. "You okay?"

"Yeah, I'm doing fine." She sat up. "But I'd like to know what's going on. Do you think you can find a weather report on the radio?"

"Sure." He threw back the blanket and got up. He grabbed his cane, went to the radio and turned it on.

"It's a good thing the cabin is powered by a generator, because I doubt this area has electricity." As the wind and rain continued to pound the cabin, he finally found a station and soon heard that there were two tornadoes spotted outside San Angelo.

Just then the cell phone rang. Dylan grabbed it off the table. "Hello." He listened, then said, "You're sure? Okay, we will. Bye." He punched the off button and frowned. "That was Chance. There's a tornado headed in this direction."

She jumped up. "Are they coming to get us?"

"No time. We need to take cover now!"

Brenna grabbed another of Dylan's shirts. "Where do we go?"

He glanced around. "Chance suggested the bathroom...the tub." He grabbed the blanket off the bed and took her hand. "Come on."

Inside the dark bathroom, Dylan led her to the tub. "Get in," he ordered.

She did as he asked, then helped him get over the side. Shivering, she huddled on the bottom. Dylan pulled her to him and wrapped the blanket around them.

"Dylan, I'm afraid," she confessed.

"I'm not going to let anything happen to us," he

promised as he laid her down in the large tub and eased himself beside her.

The sound of the wind intensified, almost deafening to the ear. Suddenly a sharp crackle sounded, then a crash against the cabin wall. Brenna gasped.

Dylan pressed his body to hers. ''Ssh, darlin'. It's going to be okay.'' His lips touched her forehead, then her cheek as the wind continued to howl.

Brenna had never been so scared. She couldn't stop trembling. She burrowed her face into Dylan's chest, trying to absorb his warmth, his strength. Then came a sound like a speeding train and they both froze. He drew her underneath him, using his body to protect her as the noise grew louder and louder and the cabin began to shudder.

''Dylan!'' she cried.

''Hang on, love. I'm not going to let you, or our baby, get hurt.'' He pulled the blanket over them as they huddled in the tub. Brenna began saying a litany of prayers to keep them safe, to let her baby be born so she could have a chance to love it, not to let anything happen to Dylan.

The cabin shook as if it was going to explode, then came the sound of glass breaking, but Dylan never let go of her.

She hoped he never would.

There was quiet. Wonderful silence, only the sound of the pouring rain as it came through the window, soaking him.

Dylan pulled back the blanket and looked down at a frightened Brenna. ''You okay?'' He was almost afraid to ask.

When she nodded, he smiled and broke the heavy tension.

"Oh, God. That was close." He managed to sit up and glance around, but he couldn't see a thing. It was pitch black and rain was coming in everywhere.

"Come on, we better find out the damage." He climbed out of the tub and helped Brenna.

"What if it isn't safe?"

"I figure the tornado hit pretty close." The cell phone rang and Dylan pulled it out of his pocket. "Hello," he said.

"Dylan, it's Chance. Are you and Brenna all right?"

"Yeah, but the cabin isn't in very good shape."

"I could care less about the cabin. It's you and Brenna we're worried about. Cade's on his way over in the 4x4 to pick up the two of you. Just hang on a few more minutes. I'll call Wyatt and let him know you're safe and on your way home."

"We'll be here." Dylan found he was shaking when he hung up. "They're coming to get us. Let's go see if there's anything left of the cabin."

He took Brenna's hand and managed to open the bathroom door and lead her into the main room of the cabin. She gasped as they eyed the destruction. A tree had come through the window and part of the roof was gone. There was water everywhere.

"Oh, this is awful," she gasped. "What if we had been in here?"

"But we weren't," Dylan assured her. "And we took cover. You're safe, I'm safe, our baby is safe."

Just then a horn honked. "That's Cade. We'll leave everything. Wyatt and I can come back tomorrow."

He went to the cupboard, pulled out a dry blanket and wrapped it around her. He wanted to carry her to the car, but no way could he manage that. Instead, he put his arm around her just as Cade's headlights lit their way through the door.

"Man, am I glad to see you two are all right." Cade climbed out and glanced around at the destruction. "Damn, looks like Jared is going to be busy a while. Come on, let's get out of here and find a drier place."

"Just take us back to the cottage," Dylan said.

"Sure you don't want to go by the house? It's closer."

Dylan shook his head. "We're anxious to get home."

"I don't blame you."

The trip seemed to take forever, but they finally made it to the cottage. After thanking Cade, Dylan limped heavily on his cane as he helped Brenna inside.

"You're going to take a warm shower. You're shivering."

Brenna couldn't argue, just headed for the bathroom. As if still dazed, she stripped off the shirt and the nightgown her mother had sent for her honeymoon. Her honeymoon. How close they'd come to…

She couldn't help thinking about what could have happened to her, to the baby and Dylan. Everyone she cared about. She stopped herself. She didn't want to care about the man. Tears flooded her eyes as she climbed into the steamy shower, then a sob racked her tired body and she gave in to her emotions and began to cry in earnest. They could have died tonight…the baby, too. The brutal reality made her knees weak. She sank against the tile wall for support, then felt herself being lifted as a pair of strong arms wrapped around her. She opened her eyes to see Dylan.

"It's okay, darlin'. I've got you." He pulled her into his arms.

"I...I thought we were going to d..." She cried, not caring that she was naked, only that Dylan was with her, holding her.

The shower spray plastered his hair against his head, his clothes were soaked. "I know," he soothed. "We're safe now. All three of us." His hand moved to her protruding stomach.

She leaned into his gentle touch, never wanting him to stop.

"Let's get you out of here." He shut off the water, then led her from the shower. She stood on the carpet as he leaned against the counter and wrapped a towel around her, keeping her close to him.

"You need to be in bed," he whispered, doing the best he could to help her to her bedroom.

Practically hopping on his good leg, Dylan turned on the small lamp on the dresser. He took out a long T-shirt from the drawer and returned to Brenna. Easing her grip on the towel, he quickly dried her, trying to be fast and efficient, trying not to linger over her shapely curves. But nothing he did stopped her shaking. Maybe he should have Wyatt take them to the emergency room. He pulled the shirt over her head and began drying her hair.

"I'm so cold," she whispered through chattering teeth.

"I'll get you warm," he promised as he pulled back the blanket and helped her climb in. Covering her up, he leaned over her and began rubbing vigorously over the blanket. He forced a smile. "How's that? Any better?"

She shook her head. "I'm...still cold."

Dylan knew he had to call Wyatt. He started to leave

when Brenna reached for him. "Please, don't leave me. Hold me…"

He looked down at his wet jeans and shirt. "I'll get you wet."

"Take them off," she said, her eyes showing her need. "Please."

He quickly pulled off his boots, then stripped off his shirt and jeans. Leaving on his damp briefs, he climbed in beside her.

Brenna went into his arms. "Oh, you're so warm," she breathed.

Dylan lay still, only holding her, but Brenna had other ideas. She shifted against him. Every soft curve of her body became intimate with his as her smooth legs moved against his rough ones. He groaned.

"Brenna…you need sleep."

She raised up, her gaze locked on his. "I need…you," she confessed.

Dylan brushed her hair away from her face. "We shouldn't do this," he said halfheartedly, aching to kiss her. He couldn't remember wanting anyone so much…ever. "I don't want you regretting anything in the morning."

"I would never regret being with you."

He was only a man. He bent his head and took her mouth in a slow, yet deliberate, kiss. He pulled back slightly, then started nibbling gently on her lower lip, trying to control his desire. He felt a lurch of excitement as Brenna returned his enthusiasm. Their kiss intensified as he forced her lips apart with his persistent tongue. She tasted like heaven. Hearing her purr, he moved against her, wanting more…needing more. He wanted to know the pleasures of her body. He cupped her breast in his hand, then ran his finger over the hard nipple through the soft cotton material. She arched closer, offering him more.

He broke off the kiss and gasped for air. "God, Bren... I want you—"

His declaration was interrupted by a loud pounding on the front door. "Damn. That's Wyatt. I'll be right back," he promised. He kissed her, then climbed out of bed. After grabbing a pair of sweats from his room, he slipped them on and had just finished tying the drawstring before he opened the door.

Wyatt pushed his way into the room. "Nice of you to give me a call to let me know you and Brenna are okay."

"Sorry. I needed to get Brenna settled," Dylan said. Hell, he kind of got distracted.

"She okay?" Wyatt asked in a quiet voice. "The baby?"

Dylan nodded. "They're both okay. Damn, but it was a rough few minutes." He shivered, trying not to think about the close call. "I don't think things could have gotten much worse."

"I know. That twister came right through the valley..." Wyatt eyed his brother closely and released a long breath. "Only you could end up in a tornado on your honeymoon."

"Yeah, right. Tonight was a little too wild, even for me." He raked a shaky hand through his hair. "Brenna was pretty shaken. I made sure she took a warm shower and got into bed."

Wyatt studied him a while. "I'm sorry that I interrupted you two."

Dylan wasn't about to tell his brother anything. Not when he didn't have a clue as to what was going on, either. "You didn't. But it has been an exhausting night. I need some sleep."

"I should get back home, too. I don't want Maura to worry." He reached out and punched Dylan in the shoulder. "Man, I'm glad you're okay. Now, go back in there and take care of your wife," he said and winked. "I'm going back to mine."

The thought echoed in Dylan's head. Brenna was his wife now. He had promised her he was going to take care of her. "Good idea. I'll tell you all about it in the morning."

Wyatt nodded. "I'll be at the rough-stock pen till noon. Now get some rest, too. 'Night," he said, then walked out.

Dylan shut the door and returned to the bedroom. He sat down on the edge of the bed. "That was Wyatt, playing big brother."

"He cares about you," Brenna whispered, unable to meet his gaze.

Dylan touched her cheek and made her look at him. "What about you? Are you okay?"

He knew she was having second thoughts about what had almost happened between them. Hell, so was he.

She hesitated. "It's just earlier…I didn't plan for that to happen."

He laughed. "I don't think either one of us did." God, he still wanted her.

She groaned. "I bet you didn't plan on getting stuck with a weepy wife one minute, and one that jumps you the next."

"Tonight shook us both. We reached out to each other. We needed to feel…alive."

A tear rolled down Brenna's cheek and something tightened around his heart. Bending down, he kissed it away. "Ssh, Bren. It's okay." He pulled her into his arms and held her. He ran a soothing hand over her back and listened to her heart beating against his chest. A few minutes later he heard her even breathing return. She had fallen asleep.

This is the first time I put a woman to sleep, he thought, knowing it was for the best. He gently laid her back down on the pillow. Unable to resist, he brushed Brenna's hair away from her face, touching her cheek. She turned into his hand. The simple act caused a yearning deep inside him, and even though he should have turned away, he couldn't seem to leave her now. But the time would come soon when he had to pack up and hit the road.

Dylan stretched out next to her on the bed and she automatically curled against him, making him yearn for sharing more than just a space in bed. He closed his eyes and released a long breath. This wasn't going to be as easy as he thought. If he knew what was good for him, he'd get the hell out of town.

Before it was too late and he couldn't leave at all.

The next morning the world was sunny again. Besides a few downed trees and the wet ground, there was no sign of the severe storm that had hit the previous night. Dylan stood on the porch and inhaled the early-spring smells. He'd been up for hours. He had to. He hadn't wanted a repeat performance with Brenna this morning. She was curled up against him when he'd awakened two hours ago. He'd decided it would be safer if he got the hell out of there. He'd busied himself with his exercises and fixed some breakfast. Brenna was still asleep, and he wasn't about to wake her.

She needed rest. His therapy could wait until later. He

stepped off the porch and headed to the barn. He had his cane, but he was trying not to use it unless he had to. If he was ever going to get back on a bull, he needed to push harder. Starting today. He was going riding, and not in the damn cart. His doctor had told him he could try things, just use good judgment.

This morning, Dylan decided he was going to saddle up Cheyenne, and he and Wyatt were going to ride out to the valley. He'd been wanting to do this since his horse had arrived six weeks ago. After being in the valley the past two days, he wasn't about to stay locked up in the cottage. No more. If he was ever going to get back on his feet—and on a bull—he had to push himself, hard.

He walked through the barn and greeted the ranch hands busy doing their morning chores. He approached Cheyenne's stall and discovered it empty, then went to find Wyatt. His search ended in the corral where his brother was checking the tack on two mounts.

"Hey, I thought the rules were you don't ride unless you saddle your own mount," Dylan repeated one of their stepfather's strict rules.

Wyatt ignored him. "Just don't get used to it. From now on, you do it yourself. I was trying to save some time." He handed Dylan Cheyenne's reins. "You sure you're up to this?"

"We'll soon find out."

"Come on then, let's get going. The guys are probably already in Mustang Valley." He climbed onto his horse, a gray gelding, and waited.

Dylan swallowed and patted his horse. "Okay, boy. Be easy, I'm not ready to dance around this morning." He grabbed hold of the horn, raised his left leg to the stirrup and pushed his booted foot through, then pulled himself up into the saddle with a grunt.

Cheyenne shifted sideways, eager to get going, and Dylan had to work to calm him, taking the time to see if his leg would work the commands. He felt stiffness in his right thigh, but he didn't give up and got Cheyenne under control.

"Ready?" Wyatt asked, giving him a questioning look.

Dylan grinned. "You better believe it."

"Well, what the hell are we waiting on?" Wyatt swung the reins around and his horse turned toward the trail. They started out slow, just an easy walk, but neither horse would put up with that.

The wind and the sunlight across Dylan's face was exhilarating. Nothing had felt so good in a long time. It had been months since he felt this free. He wasn't restricted, his movement wasn't hampered at all. Flexing his leg muscles, he gave Cheyenne commands. His injured leg ached a little, but he definitely had the strength needed to control the stallion.

When they reached the open field, they began to trot, then finally broke into a flat-out run. He glanced over his shoulder and saw Wyatt trying to keep up. Finally he pulled back on the reins and eased the animal to slow down. By the time Wyatt came up beside him, he didn't look any too happy.

"Couldn't you just take it easy your first time out?" He shook his head. "Brenna's going to have my hide if anything happens to you."

He thought about Brenna and leaving her in bed. "Nothing is going to happen. Did you see me, bro? I can ride."

Wyatt smiled. "Yeah, I'd say you can ride. But can

you slow it down a bit? I'd like to get there in one piece." Wyatt walked them through the grove of trees, then the clearing as they approached the valley…and the damage.

They were silent as they rode through the high grass. Right down the middle of the valley a section was stripped bare from the tornado. Dylan looked up toward the cabin to assess the damage that was too dark to see last night. A tree had fallen over the back side and part of the roof was gone. He shivered, not wanting to think about what could have happened to them. He looked farther up the rise and saw a line of five men on horseback. Chance, Cade, Travis, Jared and Hank. The family was here.

"Come on, they're waiting on us."

Cheyenne easily made the trek up the soggy ground to the top of the rise. "'Morning, boys," Hank greeted with a nod. He directed his attention to Dylan. "I'm sorry about yesterday. I should have gotten you two out of here." He shook his head. "But there weren't any tornado warnings in the afternoon."

"Don't worry about it."

"Glad to see you're okay," Chance said to Dylan. "How is Brenna this morning?"

"She's sleeping. I thought it was better to let her rest after last night."

"It was a helluva night," Travis joked as shook his head.

"Sorry about the cabin," Dylan said.

"Hell, it's only wood," Cade said. "We're just glad you and Brenna are all right. Besides, Jared needs something to do until May."

"Hey, speak for yourself," Jared said. "I'm not going to be getting any sleep when the baby arrives."

"I hear you, bro," Chance chimed in. "I haven't had a full night in the last three months."

"Hey, stop whining like little puppies," Hank broke in. "You love every minute of it and you know it." He looked at Dylan and winked. "Don't you and Brenna wait too long to start a family, these guys already have a head start on you."

Dylan felt the heat rise to his face. Did Hank know their situation? He doubted it. "We'll see."

"Hey, Dylan, glad to see you on horseback," Jared said. "How soon before you test out a bull?"

"Not sure. But I'll let you know."

"Hey, maybe you can invite us over to watch," Travis said, looking hopeful.

"We'll see." He found he was looking forward to it, and to spend more time with these guys. Not that he was ready to join the family, but maybe it wouldn't hurt to be friends.

Chapter Nine

She was going to kill him.

How dare he go and risk hurting himself? Brenna paced the cottage, ignoring Maura's scrutiny. She drew a breath to calm herself. It didn't work. Not when Dylan was out there doing something foolish. Well, what did she expect? The man would do anything on a dare.

"You said he went with Wyatt?" she asked.

Maura nodded. "Wyatt will make sure Dylan's careful. They wanted to see the tornado damage in Mustang Valley."

"Aunt Brenna, are you mad at Unca Dylan?" little Kelly asked.

"I'm not angry, honey, just worried. His leg isn't as strong as it should be."

"Mommy gets mad at Daddy sometimes, but then he kisses her and makes it all better. Maybe you should do that and you won't be mad anymore." The child looked hopeful.

"Aren't you just a busy little bee," her mother said.

She looked at Brenna apologetically. "And here all this time I thought she was playing with her dolls."

Just then the door opened and a smiling Dylan walked in, followed by Wyatt.

"Brenna...you're up."

She folded her arms over her breasts. "I usually am at this time of day." She glanced at the clock. It was nearly eleven. "I didn't know you were planning on going out."

"I didn't think I would be gone too long."

Maura stood and took her daughter's hand. "I think we should head back to the house, Kelly."

"But Mommy," the girl began, "I want to tell Unca Dylan something."

"What is it, sweetness?" Dylan asked as he knelt down and pulled the child to him.

Kelly's blue eyes grew large as she caught her mother's warning glare. "I gotta whisper it in your ear."

"Okay." Dylan leaned forward and listened intently as the child relayed her message. He then whispered something back that made Kelly giggle.

Then each of her parents took one of the child's hands and walked out toward the door, where Maura paused. "Why don't you two come up for dinner tonight? Jeff and Kelly will have eaten and will be upstairs watching a movie. That leaves the adults to enjoy their enchiladas."

"Sounds good," Dylan said, wishing he wasn't left alone to face Brenna.

"Don't forget, Unca Dylan," Kelly called from the porch. "Kiss her for a really, really long time like Daddy does Mommy—" The child's words were cut off when the door closed.

They were alone. Dylan waited for Brenna to say

something. She didn't, just walked into the kitchen, poured some water from the kettle into a cup and added a tea bag. She did look rested, her complexion fresh, and the color back in her cheeks. Her fiery locks lay in thick curls against her shoulders. She had on her usual baggy sweats, but now he knew what was underneath. He recalled his trip into the shower, holding her naked body in his arms.

He quickly shook away the direction of his thoughts and focused on saving his butt. "I was going to tell you, but you were sleeping so soundly," he said.

She took a sip of her tea. "You could have left me a note."

He wasn't going to waste time arguing. "You're right, I should have."

"Or maybe you knew I'd be upset that you got on a horse." She glared at him.

He raised a hand. "Hey, the doctor said I could start doing more, just not to be foolish."

"So you didn't go for a run, you walked Cheyenne all the way to the valley? Right?" She cocked an eyebrow. "What if you'd fallen?"

"I fall all the time," he said. "Remember, it's what I'm good at. Getting off an animal, fast."

Brenna knew she was being foolish. Of course Dylan had to start doing more. She recalled a time when he wouldn't even get out of his wheelchair. The reason she'd been hired had been her promise to get him back on his feet. His determination to get back on the circuit had helped them both make their goals. "You missed the therapy session."

"I know, but I thought we would make it up this afternoon."

She shook her head. "I have a doctor's appointment."

"Okay, then we go to the doctor's, come back here and do the therapy."

She couldn't believe it. Since when was he going with her? "You don't need to go with me."

He looked hurt. "I know. I'd like to though, unless you have a problem with me tagging along."

There were a hundred reason why he shouldn't, but right now she couldn't think of a single one. "I also have an ultrasound scheduled."

He smiled, and it stole her breath. "Well, hot damn. We're finally going to get a look at this little one." He walked up to her and pulled her into his arms, then placed a kiss on her mouth. She didn't have a chance to resist as the kiss quickly intensified and swept her away. When he finally pulled back, her legs could barely hold her up. He leaned his forehead against hers.

"You still angry with me?" he asked.

Unable to speak, she shook her head.

His grin broadened. "I guess Kelly was right. But maybe I should convince you a little more." He lowered his head once again and covered her mouth.

Oh, this man definitely wasn't playing fair.

That afternoon Dr. Sara Parks studied Brenna's chart. "Well, it looks like you're doing just fine," she told her. "You put on three pounds last month. Is the morning sickness easing up?"

Brenna nodded. "Yes. I haven't had any in almost two weeks."

"Good. Now that you're in your second trimester it should subside altogether." The doctor smiled. "I see here that you got married. Congratulations. Is the father here today?"

Brenna nodded, then corrected the doctor's assumption. "Dylan is going to be my baby's father, but the biological father is dead."

"I remember you telling me that." She scribbled something on the chart. "Well, I hope you and Mr. Gentry will be happy."

"Thank you, Doctor."

Just then there was a knock on the door and Dylan peered in. "How's she doing, Doc?"

"She's perfect."

He walked in. Playing the attentive husband, he stood next to the exam table and took Brenna's hand. "I think so, too, but she has a tendency to be a little bossy. Can you do something about that?"

The forty-something doctor apparently wasn't immune to Dylan's charms. "Why not let her have her way then?"

He laughed. "Good idea. Thanks."

Another knock and a pretty, blond technician wheeled in the ultrasound machine. "Picture time," she said with a bright smile aimed at Dylan.

"That's just what we've been waiting for," Dylan said and glanced at her name tag. "Renee. Our baby's first picture."

"Well, let's get started then," the tech suggested. "Lie back, Mrs. Gentry."

Brenna did as she was asked, using the pillow to prop herself up so she could see the screen.

"Mr. Gentry, you go around and stand beside your wife so you get a good view." The tech reached for a tube of cream. "Just to warn you, this cream will be a little cold." She pulled down the sheet and tugged up Brenna's gown, exposing her rounded stomach for the world to see. Well, that bit of reality should repel Dylan.

Dylan stood there stunned. He had touched her every

curve last night, every time she pressed against him. But this was the first time he actually saw the changes in her body, saw the baby growing inside her.

The machine began to make a swishing sound. "What's that?"

Renee smiled. "That is the baby's heartbeat."

Dylan's gaze went to the screen as he gripped Brenna's hand in his. The image all seemed fuzzy to him, then slowly the outline of a tiny figure came into view. He swallowed hard. It was the baby.

The tech talked with the doctor and adjusted knobs on the machine. "By the looks of it, you have yourself a very active baby."

Dylan felt Brenna trembling and he looked down and saw the tears in her eyes. "Are you okay?" he managed to ask, his own throat a little tight.

She nodded. "This just makes it all so real." Her voice was filled with awe.

"Yeah, it does." Unable to resist, he leaned down and placed a soft kiss on her forehead. His pulse raced and he wanted more, but resisted. He turned back to the machine as the technician pointed out vital parts of the baby.

"Do you two want to know the sex?" Renee asked.

Brenna looked up at Dylan and nodded. "Yes, we want to know."

"Well, let me do some investigating here. I'll go around back and in between the legs. Oh my, yes, it looks like you have yourself a girl. What do you think, Doctor? You see any equipment I've missed?"

Dr. Parks leaned toward the screen and after a few seconds smiled. "No, Renee, I have to agree with you. A girl. She should arrive sometime in mid August."

Dylan couldn't find his breath. "We're going to have

a daughter.'' He glanced at Brenna, then placed a soft kiss on her lips. ''Just what we wanted.''

''It's a girl.''

Dylan swept into the kitchen of his brother's house. Maura stood at the stove and Wyatt was setting the table for supper.

''We're having a girl.'' He waved the picture in the air.

''Hey, that's great.'' Smiling, Wyatt slapped Dylan on the back and hugged Brenna. ''Let me see.'' He took the printout from the ultrasound. ''She's a real beauty, bro. You got a name picked out?''

Dylan snatched the picture back. ''Don't make fun of the kid.''

Maura walked over. ''He's just jealous because I don't have an ultrasound scheduled until next month,'' she said as she hugged them both. ''I'm so glad everything is okay. All mothers worry about having a healthy baby.''

Just then there was a loud crash upstairs. Wyatt groaned. ''Come on, Dylan, you might as well get some practice handling kids. I need you to help me straighten this out.'' The two men left the room.

Brenna felt a little awkward. Her sister-in-law hadn't said much about the quick wedding followed by an even quicker baby announcement.

''Is there anything I can do to help with dinner?'' Brenna asked.

''You can sit down. The past few days had to wear you out.''

She sank into a chair at the kitchen table. ''I feel fine.''

Maura frowned. ''Let's see, in less than a week

you've planned a wedding, gone on a honeymoon that was interrupted by a class-four tornado, not to mention you've been working nonstop with Dylan's therapy. I know being newly married is a strain in itself." She smiled. "And with a Gentry man, to boot."

"I didn't plan on marrying Dylan," she said. "He's the one who—"

Maura sat down across from her. "Brenna, you don't owe me any explanation. I know that your baby's father died. Nothing else is any of my business. All that matters is you're married to my husband's brother and that makes you my sister." She patted Brenna's hand. "And I'm here if you ever need to talk."

A tear ran down Brenna's cheek. She'd never had a sister to talk to. "Everything happened so fast. Dylan married me because my parents demanded to know the man responsible for my baby. Before I knew it, Dylan had told them he was. He just did it because he's grateful that I'm helping him walk again." She brushed her hair away and sank back into the chair. "You must think I'm the worst person in the whole world."

Maura shook her head. "I'd never judge you. Not with my past. When I met Wyatt, I had just come from a woman's shelter. I was running away from my abusive ex-husband. You can say Wyatt rescued me and the kids. I resisted him for a long time. And in the process there're a few things I learned about Gentry men. One is they're stubborn, and another is their feelings run true and deep. They don't do things unless they want to. Brenna, Dylan cares about you…and the baby. I can see it in his eyes and I think you're perfect for him."

"I know he never wanted to get married."

"What man does? We have to convince them they can't live without us."

"What happens when Dylan goes back to bull riding? I don't know if I can handle that."

"We make a lot of sacrifices when we love someone. You gain a lot of strength, too. Dylan may surprise you and change his mind. He may find what he has here is a lot better than what he has out there on the circuit. You've seen him with Kelly. He turns to mush. Can you imagine him leaving his own daughter?"

Around nine-thirty that night Dylan and Brenna arrived back at the cottage. She was tired but too keyed up to sleep. Dylan seemed the same. She went into the kitchen and busied herself with preparing the coffeemaker for the morning. And she filled the teapot for herself.

She tried to stifle a yawn.

He came up behind her. "You should have told me you were tired. We could have come home sooner."

When Brenna turned around, he was right in front of her, looking gorgeous in his Western shirt and jeans. His hair lay in waves and was tucked behind his ears. There was still the faint scent of aftershave lingering on his skin. Her gaze raised to his silvery-blue eyes. She swallowed. "I enjoyed spending time with Maura and Wyatt. I'm fine."

"We did have a nice time, didn't we?" He smiled. "The whole day was great."

"You should be tired, too. You were up at five and on a horse for two hours, then a trip into town and waiting at the doctor's."

He leaned closer, placing an arm on either side of her head. "Best day I've had in a long time."

Brenna knew she should turn away, but she was weak

where Dylan was concerned. She wanted to be in his arms, to be held by this man, to be loved by him.

"I don't want it to end," he said in a husky voice as he lowered his head. He touched her lips tenderly, then touched them again and opened his mouth over hers and drank deeply. She whimpered.

"Easy," Dylan said, trying to rein in his eagerness. "Unless you want more?" He cocked an eyebrow. "I should warn you, if this keeps up, it's going way past kissing. Tell me you want the same."

She nodded as her arms went around his neck and her lips raised to meet his. She was an intoxicating blend of tastes and textures that left him aching for more.

"I want you, Bren... From the first day you walked in here, I've wanted you." He dug his fingers through her hair, then across her shoulders, then down her arms, eager to touch her everywhere. Her lips parted on a moan and he swallowed the sound, and his tongue thrust inside. He felt her arch against him, trying to get closer. Her eagerness nearly pushed him off balance, making him remember his vulnerability. But he couldn't get past his need for her.

He cupped her face. "I want to make love to you."

"I want that, too," she whispered back.

Silently, he took her hand and walked her to his bedroom, then closed the door. Inside, he drew her against him and reveled in the feel of her body against his as he took her mouth in a hungry kiss. It wasn't enough. His hands went under her shirt and unfastened her bra, then cupped her breasts in his hands. She shivered as he toyed with the sensitive tips until they grew hard against his fingertips. He pulled away long enough to tug off her shirt and bra, and dropped them on the floor. Then he bent down and sucked the nipple into his mouth and she groaned again as she clutched his head.

"You like that?" he asked, happy he was pleasuring her.

"Yes," she breathed.

"Then you're going to love what else I have in mind." He moved her to the bed, removing his own shirt as they went. He kissed her again and helped her kick off her shoes, then he unfastened her slacks. With an impatient tug, he let the rest of her clothes drop to the floor. Together they sank to the mattress and he laid her back against the cool sheets.

"You're beautiful," he breathed as he leaned down and stroked her breasts, then moved down to her stomach, taking great care of the new life growing inside. "You're sure it's okay for us to do this?"

She nodded. "The doctor said everything is fine. That sexual relations are good for expectant mothers." She reached for him, her mouth eager. He wrapped his arms around her, unable to get enough. He inhaled her sweet fragrance and couldn't wait any longer.

He managed to pull off his boots and socks, then stood up and worked the zipper on his jeans. "If you have any doubts, Bren...tell me now." He'd beg if he had to, but he couldn't walk away.

She reached out to him. "Make love to me, Dylan."

He was naked and beside her in no time. He drew her against him and closed his lips over hers in a shivering sigh. His hand moved over her body, touching, stroking, her, wanting to bring her pleasure.

Dylan was trembling when he parted her legs. His fingers moved in between and found her ready for him. In the dimly lit room he watched her eyes widen, then she gasped as he pushed inside her. He joined their hands as he began to move, deep, deeper until he felt he was becoming part of her.

Brenna's breath caught in her throat as Dylan's hips rocked against hers. Heat shot through her, searing her skin, burning her throat. Her body responded naturally, as if they'd made love a hundred times before. His pace picked up and she lifted her hips, searching for more as she moved with him. She wrapped her legs around his waist and arched to meet him, straining toward the pleasure.

A sob broke from her throat as he whispered sweet words against her ear and a light flashed behind her eyelids. She cried out his name as a burst of sensation swept her away. Then a low guttural sound erupted from Dylan and he collapsed on top of her.

Brenna was still floating when he drew her to his side. She never wanted to let go of him and held on tight as sleep took over.

The sun was bright the next morning. Brenna squinted as she sat up in bed. Naked. And not in her bed. Memories of last night flashed through her head. She'd made love to Dylan. Her betraying body tingled in remembrance.

It never should have happened. He was going to leave and take her heart with him. But how could she regret making love? He had been so tender, so caring. She'd never known those feelings. Never with Jason. He'd never held her after, never cared about her needs or desires.

Suddenly the door opened and Dylan came into the bedroom carrying a breakfast tray. He wore a pair of jeans and a smile. She sucked in a breath as her libido rose.

"Good morning, Mrs. Gentry."

She held the blanket against her breasts. "What time is it?"

He put the tray at the end of the bed, sat down beside her and kissed her. Not just a little peck either. A long, searing, wake-up-and-turn-you-on kiss.

Her arms went around his neck and held on. When he finally pulled away, he grinned. "Now, good morning, Mrs. Gentry."

"Good morning."

"That's better, but I'm willing to keep working to put you in a better mood."

"I'm not in a bad mood. But I just overslept. I need to get up so we can get started on your therapy."

"We can take a few minutes for breakfast." His eyes searched hers. "And for a talk. I take it you have regrets about last night."

Her chest tightened. She wanted to scream, no, that last night was the most perfect night in her life. "Looking for compliments?"

His smile died. "No, just a little honesty." He started to get up, but Brenna reached for him.

"I'm sorry, Dylan. I'm just not very good at this."

"We're married, Brenna. There's nothing wrong with what happened between us."

What about when you leave me and break my heart? she cried silently. "You know our marriage isn't real."

He looked as if she'd slapped him. "I guess you're right. My mistake." He stood. "I thought we had something special here." He grabbed a shirt and limped out of the room. A few seconds later she heard the front door slam.

Brenna wanted to go after him, but she didn't know what to say, how to explain how she felt. Who was she kidding? It was already too late to protect herself—she was totally, completely in love with the man. She looked down at the tray at the end of the bed and saw a cup of her tea and dry toast, with a dab of her favorite strawberry jam.

Brenna felt a tear slip down her cheek. Was she brave enough to take what he had to offer her? She was still afraid, but she couldn't let go of him. Not yet. They might have only a short time together, but she wanted to spend it with Dylan. She got up and headed for the shower. Now she had to convince him of that—that she and the baby both needed him.

An hour later, Brenna set out to find Dylan. He was angry with her and he had every right to be. She'd gone willingly to his bed last night and asked him to make love to her. Now she needed to tell him why she'd pulled away in the morning.

Inside the barn, the air was cooler and she had a little trouble adjusting to the dim light. Once her eyes focused, she moved through the row of stalls, seeing several horses, knowing that Dylan's horse, Cheyenne, was boarded here.

At the end of the row in the large corner stall she found the beautiful chestnut stallion. He sensed her too, and immediately stuck his head over the gate to investigate. She had to smile as she came up to him.

"Well, hello, good-lookin'. Where have you been all my life?" She reached out so the animal could sniff her hand, then she began to stroke his head. He was greedy and pushed against her, wanting more. She'd been around horses all her life, so she wasn't afraid of his aggressiveness. In fact, if she wasn't pregnant, she'd love to ride him.

"You'd better be careful. Cheyenne isn't a gentleman."

Hearing Dylan's voice, she froze, then turned around. "It's okay, I can handle him."

Carrying a bucket of feed, he moved past her, opened the gate and went inside. He finished filling the stallion's trough, patted the animal's rump and came out to face her.

"What are you doing out here?" he asked. "Do you need something?"

"Can we talk?" She glanced nervously up and down the aisle. They were alone.

His face was like stone. "What about?"

"This morning."

He shook his head. "I think you pretty much let me know how you feel—"

"No, I didn't. I got scared, Dylan." She fought hard to keep the tremble out of her voice. "I don't regret what happened last night." She sighed. "I just didn't…I didn't know how to handle it. Everything has happened so fast…" She glanced away. "But I've never once regretted marrying you, or your making love to me…even if it's the only time." She started to leave, when Dylan grabbed her arm, then backed her up against an empty stall.

This woman had Dylan at the end of his patience. "You can't say something like that and just walk away." His face was inches from hers. "I don't think so." He took her mouth in a slow, drugging kiss. She tasted heavenly, and he needed her more than his next breath. "You know how to turn me every way but loose, don't you?"

"I'm not trying to."

"The hell you aren't." He pressed against her, his

mouth on her neck, then moved to her ear, feeling her squirm. "Come on. We need some privacy to finish this discussion."

He took her by the hand and they walked back to the house. When they reached the cottage, Brenna pulled away and crossed to the other side of the living room. "Stay there," she ordered him. "First, I need to finish what I came to tell you."

He did as she asked.

She raised her chin. "I didn't plan on last night happening."

He had. "It was inevitable from the first kiss."

She looked surprised at his comment. "The point is, things have changed between us. Do you want to stay married to me?"

He blinked. If she only knew. "Yes."

She nodded. "And I want to stay married to you, but I want you to know that I won't try to stop you from going back on the circuit. And as we agreed, in six months we can decide if we want to continue or…dissolve the marriage."

He nodded. "But, Bren, no matter what happens between us, I will be there for the baby."

She stared at him. "You don't have to be if—"

Dylan was across the room and enfolded her in a tight embrace, his hand on her stomach.

"This baby—this little girl is going to have a father. So stop being so stubborn. We can make this work, Bren. Trust me."

Oh, she wanted so much to believe him. But trust? That was the problem.

Chapter Ten

Two weeks later, Dylan awoke with Brenna's naked body pressed against his side. For never having shared a bed with a woman for longer than a few hours, he was getting pretty attached to having his wife next to him, and couldn't imagine not having her there.

He placed his palm over her rounded stomach. They'd been married just three weeks, and in that time he'd watched her body change daily. He'd gotten to know her, too. Her moods, her stubbornness, her tenderness. Also where she liked to be kissed, the sounds she made when he pleasured her, and he couldn't seem to get enough of her.

Brenna shifted in her sleep and her hand stroked his chest, arousing him. He resisted the urge to turn into her touch, knowing she needed her rest, and he needed to get up.

It was time to make some plans, he thought. His agent had called him about an offer from Tom Jarvis of Extreme Thrills, a company that handled promotion for rodeos. Tom had heard about Dylan's quest to return to competition. Jarvis wanted him to make personal appearances for the upcoming rodeos and would pay him top dollar just to shake hands and sign autographs. Dylan wasn't sure he wanted to sell himself that way. And he wasn't too eager to leave home right now.

He looked down at his wife. Oh, no, he was happy right where he was. Brenna moaned and moved against him, then finally opened her eyes and smiled.

"Good morning," Dylan said and bent down and kissed her.

She wrapped her arms around him. Slowly she came to life, her legs shifting as he moved against her.

"Mmm," she sighed. "I love how you say good morning."

He kissed her again. "Oh, I'm only getting started," he said, erasing everything else from his mind.

An hour later, Dylan walked toward the rough-stock pens. As he arrived, he heard some commotion. He quickened his step and found his brother, his stock manager, Bud, along with a half-dozen hands around the corral gate looking into the pen.

"What's going on?" Dylan asked.

Wyatt turned and smiled. "Dylan, just the man I want to see. Bud bought a new bull."

Dylan stepped up to the railing and glanced at the new addition. The jet-black Brahma circled the dirt area nervously, snorting and shaking his head. The bull stood still as his ebony eyes locked with Dylan's, then he began clawing his hoof in the ground as if sending out a challenge.

Dylan was mesmerized by the huge beast. For the first

time in a long time, he felt a familiar stirring inside him. The chance to ride, to try to conquer this guy.

"What do you think of him?" Wyatt asked. "You think Tornado Alley will be any good?"

Dylan cocked an eyebrow. "Who gave him that name?"

Wyatt raised a hand. "I swear, he was already named when I got him."

"Has anyone ridden him?"

Wyatt shook his head. "We were going to try today."

Just then Brenna's younger brother, Connor, the youngest of the Farren boys, came out of the barn. Wyatt had hired the eighteen-year-old to work weekends with the horses while he finished high school.

"Hey, Connor, how's it going?" Dylan asked.

The tall, lean teenager smiled, reminding him of Brenna. "Hey, Dylan." He strolled over with a lanky gait. "Good to see you. Where's Brenna?"

"She's up at the cottage." He'd left her in bed after they'd made love. He'd hated to leave her, but she could use the extra sleep.

"You come to take a look at the new bull?"

Dylan's attention was once again drawn to the huge animal in the pen. "Yeah, I did."

"I bet you'd love to ride him," Connor teased.

Wyatt stepped in. "Ah…Dylan isn't ready to get back on a bull yet." He looked at his brother. "Don't you need to get a doctor's okay to ride?"

That could happen soon. Dylan had an appointment with his doctor that afternoon. He was tired of playing the invalid. "No, I feel fine. I wouldn't mind finding out if Tornado is worth what you paid for him."

Brenna was used to having more to do, but Dylan seemed to think that she needed a lot of sleep. She didn't. And staying cooped up all day in the cottage was making her crazy, especially since her husband didn't need her help as much anymore.

He could drive his truck now. Besides, he had been riding Cheyenne nearly every day. Because of her pregnancy, she couldn't ride a horse with him. Finished with the little housework there was, she was pretty bored by the inactivity. Maybe she'd ask Dr. Morris about taking on another patient. Part-time, of course.

Brenna knew all too well that her future could change suddenly. Dylan had never promised her he'd settle down and she found she needed more of a commitment than just that he would hang around for six months.

What about after?

Would he go out on the circuit and she'd stay at home and discover that she couldn't take it? What about all the beautiful, willing women who chased after rodeo stars? Could she compete when her stomach was so large she couldn't tie her shoelaces? How could he still desire her then?

She thought back to just hours ago when he'd made love to her, and last night he'd been just as eager. A shiver went through her body at the memory. She had to stop with the doubts. Dylan was here with her now and he had promised that he would always be there for the baby.

Brenna grabbed her coat and left the cottage. She needed some fresh air, and since her brother, Connor, was working for Wyatt today, she could go visit him. She walked through the deserted barn wondering where everyone was, then she heard the loud voices and cheers coming from the rough-stock pens.

That was probably where she would find both Dylan

and Connor. She smiled, thinking about the time her husband had spent with her family. Her brothers all looked up to him. Her happiness suddenly evaporated when she came out of the barn and saw Dylan at the top of the chute just about to climb onto a bull. Her heart lodged in her throat and her entire future began to fade away. He was joking with the other ranch hands, when he abruptly glanced over at her.

She couldn't handle this, not again. She couldn't just stand here and watch as something happened to him. She swung around and marched off, ignoring Dylan calling to her, and kept walking until she made it back to the cottage.

Once inside, she wanted to hide, wanted to forget what she'd seen at the pens. But the image of Dylan sitting on top of the bull wouldn't go away.

The door opened and Dylan walked into the room. "Brenna, you can't ignore me."

"I don't feel like talking."

"That's exactly what we need to do. Let me explain."

"You don't owe me any explanation," she told him. "From the beginning, you said your goal was to go back on the circuit. Well, congratulations, it looks like you're about to make it."

"I didn't do anything," he said. "I wasn't going to ride, I was just showing another rider some tips on how to grip the rigging."

She blinked rapidly. "And you *needed* to climb into the chute on top of a bull to do that?"

"Maybe not," he hedged. "But, dammit, I needed to get up there for myself. To see if I could do it. It's been seven months since my accident. Maybe I wanted to know if I'd lost my nerve."

She wished he had.

"Dammit, Bren, you always knew my plans were to get back on a bull."

Oh, yes, she knew. But she was hoping she would matter more. Wrong again. "Fine, then why don't you stop talking about it and just go?"

He looked as if she had slapped him. "Is that the way you want it?"

She didn't have a choice. "That's the way I want it."

That afternoon Dylan sat in Dr. Morris's exam room while Brenna stayed at the cottage.

"Well, it looks good," the white-haired doctor said as he clipped the film onto the lighted viewing screen. "You've healed nicely. I can't believe you're the same man who was wheeled in here months ago. I'd say your recovery is nothing short of remarkable. And I'd also say that your excellent physical therapy is the reason why." He smiled. "Of course, I don't have to tell you how vital Brenna's been to your success. You married her. Where is she today?"

"I can drive now, so she stayed at home," he lied. He hadn't asked her to come along.

"I guess I don't need her here since I have her chart on your progress." He shook his head. "You know, Dylan, I didn't have much hope for you when I got your case. Especially with your attitude and your ability to chase off therapists. Brenna was just about your last hope. She was the only one who wouldn't give up on you. I can see why you wanted to keep her around."

Dylan felt as if a knife had pierced his heart. "Yeah, she's been a real workhorse, and kept me in line." He couldn't talk about her anymore. "Doctor, I want to know about going back on the circuit. Am I ready?"

The older man studied the chart again. "You've regained close to eighty-five percent of your leg strength, but most likely you'll always have a slight limp. That could get better, or worse, especially when the weather gets cold.'' He sighed. ''I'm not crazy about you bull riding, but there's no medical reason why you can't return.''

Dylan nodded. After waiting so long, the day had finally come, and now he wasn't sure it was what he wanted to hear. He stood and shook the doctor's hand. ''Thank you for giving me back my life.''

The older man smiled. ''You're welcome, but I'm not the person you need to thank. Save your gratitude for your wife.''

Yes, he owed Brenna a lot. And wished he could give her what she needed—a husband who would be around all the time.

Dr. Morris signed the chart, then added, ''There's one more thing, Dylan. I need to stress that if you go back to bull riding, that steel rod in your leg doesn't make you a superhero. You could fall or land at a funny angle and there is a chance that you'd injure your leg again. And you may not be so lucky the next time. Maybe you should think about what's more important.''

The doctor left and Dylan went to the waiting room and Wyatt.

''Well, how did it go?'' his brother asked.

''Fine. I'm good to go.''

''And just where are you plannin' to go?''

''Where I've always planned. Back on the circuit.''

Wyatt raised an eyebrow. ''What about Brenna and the baby?''

''Brenna and I have discussed this and she knows the score. In fact, she encouraged me to go. So I'm heading out on a promotional tour on the Texas circuit.''

"Are you going to ride?"

"I haven't decided yet." He definitely needed practice before that happened.

"You don't have to, bro. I think Brenna would be happy if you told her you'd decided to stick around. I know I would be. The partnership offer is still on the table."

Dylan laughed as they walked out of the medical building. "Hey, remember I'm like our old man, Jack. I'm too restless to be cooped up. I need excitement. I need to be out there on the road, doing what I'm good at."

Even though Brenna had become important to him, how long could he stay at the ranch? What if he couldn't give her what she needed? God, he couldn't stand seeing disappointment in her eyes, knowing he wasn't the man he wanted to be. Until he climbed back on a bull, he was still in limbo.

Wyatt stared at him. "You've never tried anything else. You might surprise yourself."

"Yeah, and I could fail, too."

Six days later, Dylan sat in his hotel room in Lubbock, Texas, staring at the telephone. He'd been gone nearly a week and he was miserable. He was back in the limelight, but it wasn't the same. He hadn't gotten on a bull. He was only on display. So far, the promoter had used his name and past championships to help bring in the crowds. Years ago, Dylan would have loved the attention, the women and the free rounds of drinks everyone wanted to buy a world champion.

And there were the endless questions from reporters. The first and foremost was, "Are you coming back?" The second one was, "Are you as good as before?" A lot of the other bull riders asked the same things. For the first time in a long time, he wondered if he could survive the eight-second ride. Did he even have the determination and courage to get back on a bull?

Not when all he could think about was Brenna. Was she eating and taking care of herself? She'd had a doctor's appointment yesterday. How was the baby? Growing, no doubt. Brenna would be, too. He remembered her rounded stomach, the feel of her soft skin under his hands. Suddenly frustrated, he stood and walked to the window. Dammit, he had to stop thinking about her. All she had to do was ask him to stay. Instead, she'd pushed him away—out of her life, out of the baby's life.

He had talked with Wyatt, but his brother hadn't been real forthcoming in giving him any information. He just told Dylan to call Brenna. What if she wouldn't talk to him? Oh hell, he'd be back home in another week.

Home.

It surprised him how much he had begun to think about the Rocking R that way. Especially since Wyatt's offer to sell him part of the ranch kept nagging at him. Kept him thinking about building a home, a place for Brenna and the baby. What if he failed? What if he couldn't be what she needed? Be the man she deserved? He had to prove to himself he could be the man he once was.

There was a knock on the door. He got up and looked through the peephole to find Ty Andrews, one of the young, up-and-coming bull riders on the circuit. He opened the door.

The guy grinned. "Hey, Dylan."

"Hi, Ty. Nice riding today."

"Thanks to you. I drew a good bull and remembered a few tricks you taught me."

"It's your talent. What can I do for you?"

"Just wonderin' if you want someone to help you with practice. If you're not busy tomorrow morning, my dad's place is a few miles west of here. He has a few Brahmas and a practice chute. He helps coach me and maybe…you might want to try to ride."

Dylan froze. Here was the chance he'd been waiting for. "I'm not sure," he hedged. "I didn't plan on riding this trip." Yeah right, then why had he brought his rigging?

"Okay. I understand if you're not ready." He turned to leave, when Dylan called him back.

"Hey, wait a minute." He took a breath. "Why don't we talk about it over some dinner."

"Sure," Ty said.

"A steak sounds pretty good and I'm going to let you buy." Dylan slipped into his boots, then grabbed his wallet off the dresser.

Ty countered. "Then you buy the drinks."

Dylan agreed. Maybe a few drinks would chase a beautiful redhead out of his mind.

"Are you sure you're okay?" Wyatt asked. "Do you need anything?"

The following weekend Brenna sat at the kitchen table at the ranch house. Both Maura and Wyatt insisted she come up for supper. "Yes, Wyatt, I'm fine. And no, I don't need a thing." Except for her husband to come home, she thought.

"Then why are you working in your condition?"

"I'm pregnant, Wyatt, not helpless. Besides, I'm only helping out Dr. Morris a few hours a day. I have a lot of time on my hands."

''Dammit, Brenna. Dylan should be here to take care of you.''

''No. I don't need to be taken care of. And Dylan is where he wants to be.''

''How long is it going to take before you two realize that you belong together?''

How she wished that were true. ''Look, Wyatt. I went into this marriage knowing the rules.''

He shook his head. ''The rules can change. I've never seen Dylan as happy as when he's with you.''

She'd thought he was happy, too.

''You should have said you didn't want him to leave. Told him how you feel.''

''Wyatt,'' Maura called as she walked into the kitchen. ''The kids want you to come upstairs to say good-night.''

''I'll be there in a minute.''

''Honey, I think it's best to go *now*,'' Maura stressed as she came to the table. ''I'll get Brenna some tea and keep her company while you're gone.''

Reluctantly, Wyatt got up and left the room.

Maura carried two cups to the table. ''Sorry. He's been like this since Dylan left. He feels responsible for allowing it. Since it was his bull…''

Brenna didn't blame anyone. ''I knew from the start that Dylan was going back to rodeoing. Oh, Maura, I never should have let this get out of control. I should have told my parents the truth from the beginning. Dylan only married me because he thought he could help my situation.'' Her voice lowered. ''He was grateful that I got him to walk.''

''You did get Dylan to walk when the rest of us failed, but I don't think most men marry out of gratitude. From the beginning, Dylan has been attracted to you.''

Brenna glanced down at her protruding stomach. "Yeah, I'm a real sex goddess."

"To him you are."

Brenna knew that was true. Dylan had been fascinated by the baby growing inside her.

Maura smiled. "A lot of men think pregnant women are sexy. Besides, I think Dylan isn't as shallow as he's let everyone believe. He says he doesn't want to settle down, or to have a permanent home. Have you ever thought that was because he's never had one? Wyatt and Dylan lived out of a single-wide trailer until they were ten. Their stepfather let them know from the day he married their mother that they weren't welcome in his home. Then just this past year, they learned that a womanizing jerk named Jack Randell was their biological father."

Brenna's chest tightened as she listened to the sad story.

"No wonder Dylan is so crazy about the rodeo," Maura said. "Everyone there loves him, but at the same time, he doesn't think he has any worth unless he risks his life and climbs on a bull to give them an eight-second thrill."

Wyatt returned to the room and sat down next to his wife. "And I'd give anything to get Dylan to retire and come work with me. Chance, Cade and Travis have approached him to open a bull-riding school and be a partner in the Mustang Valley Guest Ranch." Wyatt frowned, and Brenna realized how much he looked like his twin. "All my life, all I ever wanted was a home." He took hold of Maura's hand. "But Dylan ran from it. Then you came along...and the baby. When he told me he was going to marry you, I was floored. This is a man who's never made any kind of commitment. But he was ready to be your baby's father. Does that give you any idea how he must feel about you?''

Brenna swallowed.

"Now," Wyatt continued, "getting him to admit it is another thing, but he was making a start.''

Maura looked up at her husband and smiled. "The Gentrys are a little hardheaded.''

"I beg your pardon," Wyatt said. "If I remember, you were the one who needed convincing. I wanted to marry you. You ran off and I had to chase you down.''

She kissed him, then turned back to Brenna. "So I was a little afraid to trust again. But as you can see, Wyatt did finally convince me.''

"It's different with you two," Brenna said. "Dylan doesn't love me.''

Maura's eyes lit up. "The man is crazy about you and your unborn child.''

Brenna wanted to believe her. "Then why did he leave?''

Wyatt was the one who answered. "It has nothing to do with you. He needs to prove something to himself.''

Brenna didn't need Dylan to prove anything to her unless it was that he loved her. In return, maybe she needed to show him that she would stand by him, too. But was she strong enough to handle Dylan being a bull rider? Could she watch her husband as he did what he loved to do?

There wasn't the slightest doubt. Yes, she could. She wanted to be with Dylan. Or was it too late?

"Wyatt, where is Dylan now?''

"He's headed for Fort Worth this weekend.''

She sighed. "So far.''

"Not too far. If need be, I can get you there.''

"How?''

"Cade Randell has a plane," Wyatt said. "I bet he'd fly us to Fort Worth, unless you can't because of the baby."

"That shouldn't be a problem, but I'll call the doctor and check. And you call Cade to see if he'll take us."

"There's something else," Wyatt began. "Dylan's entered in the bull-riding event tomorrow. Can you handle that?"

Brenna tensed. She didn't know that Dylan was going back so soon. She was suddenly sad that he felt he couldn't share that with her. "If the doctor says I can fly, I'm going."

Wyatt grinned. "You're making the right decision."

She sure hoped so. Dylan might already think she wasn't worth all the trouble. Somehow she needed to convince him that no matter what, she'd be there waiting for him when he came home.

Chapter Eleven

Saturday morning, Dylan wasn't at the rodeo just to sign autographs. He was entered in the bull-riding event. A year ago, he would have loved all the attention from the fans for his attempted comeback—especially from the women—but today he just wanted to be left alone. He needed to concentrate on the job he had to do. The last thing he wanted was to play celebrity.

So many things had changed since he'd met Brenna. The main thing was they were married. And right now he wanted desperately to talk to her, just to hear her voice. So much so he wanted to pack up and go, but he couldn't think about the future until he dealt with the past.

The last five days, Dylan had been at Ty Andrews's family's ranch to see if he could get back into competitive shape. He'd started out bad, then it got worse. He couldn't stay on the bull, Doctor Dread, much past the gate opening. It hadn't been easy, and he'd felt every jar and buck, but Dylan needed to get his strength and balance back. Mainly to see how his leg handled the landings. Maybe he was past his prime. But he couldn't walk away yet. He had one more thing to do.

Since today's rodeo was small, and not many of the big names were there, it gave Dylan the perfect opportunity to check his ability. This was his chance to see if he still had it. To see if he could still handle a real competition.

Dylan heard the announcer start the bull-riding event and he headed toward the chutes. Before he got there, he heard his name called out. He turned around and saw a woman who looked familiar. It took a moment, then her name came to him. Lisa Sue Hartley. The pretty blonde showed up at lot of rodeos. She particularly liked bull riders. They'd hooked up a few times, but it had never been anything serious.

With a big smile she strolled toward him, dressed in tight Wranglers and a multicolored Western shirt. Her Stetson sat perfectly on her blond head. She wasn't shy, either, and planted a kiss on his mouth. He managed to back away, but she was persistent and wanted to meet him later. Not long ago he would have been eager to party with her, but the invitation was no longer appealing. All he could think about was Brenna and his upcoming ride.

"I need to get to the chute, I'm up soon." He took off for the pens and found Ty waiting for him. He handed Dylan his rigging and wished him luck. Dylan felt the nerves as he adjusted his chaps, but he liked knowing that the adrenaline was flowing.

"You'll do just fine." The young rider slapped him on the back. "Just remember, you're the best in the world. You don't need to prove anything."

Yeah, he could walk away now, but he knew he

couldn't go back to Brenna if he wasn't whole. Not until all his demons were conquered. "I need to prove something to myself."

Dylan worked rosin along the rigging, then climbed up the outside of the chute and straddled the top rail. He'd drawn a gray bull named Ornery Critter. Dylan hung the bell-weighted rope down the side, then the worker across from him hooked and pulled it up around the animal's flank and tied it. Dylan tugged at his gloves and sucked in a breath, then swung his leg over and took a seat on the back of the bull.

Ignoring the snort of the thousand-pound animal under him, Dylan went on with the ritual and slid his hand up and down under the rigging, then wrapped the rope around his hand and made a tight fist. He shoved his hat down on his head and shut out the crowd noise when they announced his name.

This was it. It was all or nothing. And he wanted it all. He wanted his life back. He sat up straight, raised his hand in the air, then called out, "go" and gave a nod. The gate swung and Ornery shot out.

The bull immediately went into a tight turn, then stopped and reversed direction. Dylan anticipated the move, but only for a split second. Ornery was known for his high kicks and Dylan wasn't disappointed as he fought to keep his balance and not fall forward. He'd lost his hat, but not his seat. Miraculously, he landed square on the bull's back and stayed with the animal as he changed direction once again. Ornery went into a series of high kicks and still Dylan kept his balance.

Then the buzzer went off.

The crowd roared as Dylan hit the ground and rolled away from danger, then scrambled to his feet. The clowns went to work and waved their arms to attract the bull's attention. Dylan ran to the fence, where he was swept through the gate to safety.

The announcer came over the loudspeaker. "Looks like 'The Devil' is back." Then a score of ninety-three was posted by the judges and a loud cheer erupted through the crowd.

Dylan hadn't even caught his breath when Ty came up. "Nice goin'." He handed him his hat. "We both made the final round."

None of that mattered to Dylan. All he cared about was he'd gotten back on the bull and rode the full eight seconds. He didn't need any more buckles or championships.

Just then Lisa Sue reappeared next to him, bringing along the newspeople eager to get pictures of the two of them. Dylan wanted to be by himself. Lisa felt differently and placed a kiss on his mouth. He jerked back. "Don't, I'm married."

She looked surprised. "Why isn't she here to see you ride?"

A longing tugged at him, and he wished Brenna were here to watch him. "She's pregnant. And it's better for her to stay home." That's where he wanted to be, too.

The blonde's hands went up the front of his shirt. "Then I say you could use some attention."

He gently removed her hands. "No, thanks," he said just as he heard his name called out.

Dylan looked up and saw Wyatt coming through the crowd of people. What was his brother doing here? Oh, God. Was something wrong with Brenna? The baby? Then he saw her. Brenna. Dylan's breath caught in his throat. It had only been two weeks, but he was hungry for the sight of her. She looked so pretty with those big brown eyes and pert nose.

He pulled free from Lisa and went to his wife. "Bren," he called. "What are you doing here?"

"I came see you. But I can see you don't need me here."

"Bren, that's not true." Dylan reached for her, but she pulled away. "Let me explain. I did know Lisa from before, but there's nothing going on..." He forced a smile. "You really came here to watch me ride?" That thrilled him.

"It was a mistake."

"No, don't leave," Dylan said. "We can go somewhere and talk."

She shook her head, then turned to Wyatt. "I'll meet you at the car." She walked off.

"Bren...hear me out."

Wyatt grabbed him before he could leave. "Just let her be, Dylan. She isn't ready to listen right now."

"But I need to tell her I didn't do anything. I know I had a reputation, but I swear, Wyatt, since I married Brenna I've never so much as looked at another woman. I'm crazy about her."

"Then you should have let her know how you felt before running off."

"Hell, I didn't even know how I felt until I left. I didn't know how much I'd miss her. Is she okay?"

"She's miserable." Wyatt glanced over his shoulder. "Look, I need to go after her. Cade flew us here, so I'll have her home in a few hours." He started off, then stopped. "Just so you know. Brenna came here to support you. She realized how much you love bull riding and she wants you to be happy."

Dylan couldn't feel any worse. And it was his own fault. He'd gone after what he wanted, hadn't he? It was all he'd been working for. The rodeo was his life. Then he'd found Bren… God, she was beautiful, stubborn, sexy, bullheaded and he loved her. He blinked at the realization. When had it happened that he couldn't stop thinking about her, couldn't stop wanting her every night, wanting to see her smile every morning.

Ty appeared. "Want to grab some food before the finals?"

Dylan came out of his reverie. "No, I'm not going to be around for the finals."

Ty cocked an eyebrow. "Why? You get hurt?"

Surprisingly his leg felt pretty good. "No. I found something I want more. I just need to convince her of that."

Ty grinned. "Good luck." He shook Dylan's hand. "It's nice that you could go out on top."

Dylan didn't feel on top. In fact, he'd never felt so low.

Brenna hadn't slept all night. That morning she called Dr. Morris and told him she couldn't make it in to work. She really needed to get her things together so she could be gone before Dylan returned. With no other choice, she had to live with her parents. Not for long though. She had money saved and if she could continue to work, she should be able to make it.

She took her clothes from the dresser and placed them in a suitcase. Dylan could file for divorce, and of course, she wouldn't contest it, or hold him to any promises. A tear found its way down her cheek. Then that part of her life would be closed…for good.

She sank to the bed. She couldn't do this anymore. Once again, she'd allowed another man to break her heart. This time was even worse than before. What she'd felt for Jason had been infatuation. She truly loved Dylan. But no more. From now on, it was going to be her and her baby.

"Bren…"

At the sound of her name, she jerked around. Dylan stood in the doorway. Oh, God. Why did he have to see her like this? "If you give me ten minutes I'll be out of here."

"So you're just going to walk out on us?"

She gathered her pride and looked at him. "We both know this marriage was a mistake. You don't need a wife tying you down. And by the looks of the way you rode yesterday, you'll be back doing what you love." She straightened. "It's what I promised you, it's what you paid me for."

Dylan was so tired. He'd driven all night to get back. He hadn't had any sleep, and he was wearing the same clothes from his ride. But seeing Brenna packing, he didn't care a damn about how he felt.

"Look, Bren…I left the rodeo right after you did and I drove all night. Have mercy on a guy and let me take a shower. Then we can talk."

"We've talked, Dylan. It hasn't done us any good. Just admit we made a mistake so we can move on. Maybe we can remain friends."

"Friends?" Dylan shot across the room. "You want to forget everything that's happened between us?" He grabbed her by the arms and pulled her close. Before she could protest, his mouth covered hers. The familiar hunger was there as her lips parted and he tasted her, praying it wouldn't be the last time. She whimpered and slipped her arms around his neck and his desire soared higher. She was his. He couldn't let her go.

He broke off the kiss. "Please, Bren…just let me

clean up and get some coffee down me so I can think straight.''

Brenna nodded. She couldn't speak. She'd already shown him too much of her feelings. She was weakening and that was bad. This man could talk her into anything and promise her anything except what she truly needed from him. His love.

He kissed her again and selfishly Brenna let him, savoring the feel of him against her, her body responding eagerly, knowing this was the last time. Then when he went into the shower she gathered up the rest of her clothes and walked out the door, wondering how she was going to survive not seeing him again.

An hour later, Dylan rushed through the back door of Wyatt and Maura's house to find his brother sitting at the table with Jeff and Kelly.

''Is Brenna here?''

Wyatt shook his head. ''No, should she be?''

Dylan glanced down at a concerned Kelly. ''Hello, sweetie.''

''Hi, Unca Dylan. Did you lose Aunt Brenna?''

''Yeah, honey. I sure did.''

''Hi, Uncle Dylan,'' Jeff greeted. ''Did you win a buckle at the rodeo?''

''Not this time, buddy.'' He tousled the boy's hair, then looked at his brother. ''I need to find her.''

Wyatt looked at his kids. ''Jeff, why don't you and Kelly go watch some television.''

''You need to talk, huh?'' The four-year-old nodded, then climbed down from the chair and hugged Dylan. ''I hope you find her so you won't be so sad.'' The little girl took her brother's hand and they walked out of the room.

Dylan raked his fingers through his hair. "Wyatt, you've got to help me. Brenna left me."

"Did you tell her you wanted her to stay?" Maura stood at the kitchen door. "Sorry, I shouldn't interrupt."

"No!" Dylan gasped and went to her. "Please, I need help to get Brenna back."

"Then you have to decide what you're going to offer her. Is it going to be her waiting here while you're off rodeoing and kissing other women?"

"Lisa Sue kissed *me*," he insisted. "I didn't kiss her. My only objective was getting on that bull yesterday to see if I could ride him. Afterward, I discovered that I didn't need that any more. I want Brenna and the baby. I want us to be a family."

"Then convince *her* you're going to stick around, not us."

Suddenly an idea stuck Dylan. He looked at his brother. "You got time to go for a drive?"

"Sure," Wyatt said. "Where we headed?"

"Could you show me that land you offered to sell to me? Unless you've changed your mind about us being partners."

Grinning, Wyatt got up, headed for the door and grabbed his hat. "Come on, there's a sweet spot that would be perfect to build you a house."

"Just what I want." Inside he was praying that Brenna would want his love. Because he'd decided he couldn't live without her.

Brenna didn't feel like getting out of the house, but her mother insisted that they go into town for lunch. So Brenna had gotten dressed in the only pants that fit her expanding waistline, her black stretch pants and an over-size blue shirt. She didn't mess with her hair, just pulled it back into a ponytail, and put on some makeup for the trip.

It had been a week since she'd left the cottage and not a word from Dylan. Brokenhearted, all she wanted to do was stay in her bedroom, but as painful as it was to think about a life without Dylan, she had to make some plans for her and her baby's future.

"Mom, would you go with me to look for an apartment?"

Maggie Farren reached across the truck seat and took hold of her daughter's hand. "Brenna, you know you don't have to move out. At least wait a while before you do anything rash."

"Mom, I need to do this," she said, knowing how easy it would be to stay. She glanced out the window and realized they were driving by the road to the Rocking R Ranch. Her home. She shook off the thought. "I need to be in my own place. I can't expect you and Daddy…" When she came home she'd told her parents everything about Jason…and Dylan.

Just then Maggie Farren turned off the highway onto a dirt road. "Hang on, it might be a little rough."

Brenna grabbed the handle over the door. "Where are we going?"

"I'm picking up your father."

"Daddy's here?" What was her father doing on Wyatt Gentry's land?

Just then they came to a clearing where Brenna saw the trailer. Dylan's trailer. The canvas awning was pulled out, shading the structure from the sun. His dusty black truck was parked under a tree. About fifty yards away, she saw two men, her father and…Dylan. Her mother pulled to the side of the road, then looked at her daughter. "Go tell your father we need to get home."

Brenna didn't want to leave the safety of the truck. "Mom, please."

"Brenna, you can't keep running. You have to face Dylan sooner or later."

Reluctantly, she climbed out of the cab and started down the slope of the hill toward the two most important men in her life. They both turned to her as she approached. Her dad smiled, but when she glanced at Dylan her breath caught in her throat as she felt his hot gaze on her.

"Bren…" he whispered.

"Hello, Dylan." She turned away. "Daddy, Mom says we need to get home."

The tall man looked up the hill, then turned back to Dylan. "Give me a minute." Before Brenna could do anything, her father took off jogging to the truck, leaving her alone with Dylan.

She didn't think she could hurt any more, but she was wrong. At the sight of this man, her chest tightened painfully. He looked so good. His Wrangler jeans were creased down the front. His colorful Western shirt of blue and white brought out the azure hue in his eyes. His cowboy hat tipped low on his head, shading the sun.

She started to go, but Dylan stopped her.

"Please, Bren, don't go," he pleaded.

"I have to." She waved her hand. "My parents need to get home." Just then she glanced toward the truck and saw her mother turning around. They were leaving her. Oh no, her parents had set her up.

She began to hurry up the slope, but by the time she reached the road, they were gone. "Darn it. Why did they leave me?"

"Because I asked them to," Dylan said from behind her.

She glared at him, then turned away. She wouldn't cry.

"Okay, Bren, I'll take you back. I only asked your parents to give me a chance to talk with you. I would never hold you here against your will."

She closed her eyes. It hurt to look at him. "We've said everything, Dylan."

"No, we haven't." He blew out a long breath. "Can you at least tell me how you're feeling?"

"There's no need for you to worry, I'm fine."

"But I do worry. You're carrying my baby." His gaze went to her stomach and she felt a warmth spread through her.

She gasped. "Don't say that."

"Why not? I told you that I was going to be here for her. I don't go back on my word."

She couldn't listen anymore. "Will you please take me home?"

"Yes, but after I show you something." He raised a calming hand. "I promise it won't take any longer than two minutes. It's right over here."

When she nodded, he took her by the arm and they walked past the trailer. Curiosity got her and Brenna couldn't help but ask, "You're not living at the cottage?"

"No, I decided to move out here a few days ago."

Dylan had fallen in love with this spot the second Wyatt showed this land to him. The view had sold him. Together they walked to the edge of the rise that looked over the green valley trimmed with rolling hills. Several trees covered the area, which would give them plenty of shade from the summer heat.

"Do you like it?"

Brenna sighed and began taking in the scenery. "Oh, Dylan, it's spectacular."

That made him smile. "I can't tell you how happy that makes me."

"Why? Why should that matter to you?"

Hunger rose in him, and longing. He stuffed his hands in his pockets to keep from reaching for her. Once he touched her, he was gone. He needed to keep his distance, at least for now.

"Because I'm planning on building a house here. Wyatt sold me part of the Rocking R."

She blinked those incredible whiskey-colored eyes. "You're going to stay here in San Angelo?"

He nodded. "And build a permanent home." He glanced over the property. "I've been thinking about it for a while now. Wyatt has been trying to get me to move here for the last year. The Randells want me to open a bull-riding school and be part of the Mustang Valley Guest Ranch. I decided it's time."

Her eyes widened. "But you're back on the circuit. To compete."

He shook his head. "I've decided to retire."

"But your leg is fine."

"My leg isn't the problem, it's my heart. Oh, I'm not saying that I didn't need to get back on the bull. I needed to prove that I hadn't lost my edge, or my courage. Winning was important, but not as important as trying again. Can you understand that?"

She nodded. "Why didn't you say anything?"

He shrugged. "I didn't know until I'd actually climbed back onto the bull and rode, until the eight-second bell went off. Then I realized that I could walk away. No regrets."

Tears filled her eyes. "Oh, Dylan."

He wanted to go to her, but he couldn't yet. He still needed to plead his case. "I discovered I wanted something else more. You."

Brenna shivered at his words. "Oh, Dylan. For how long? Until another blonde comes along?" She hated sounding so jealous.

"If you're talking about Lisa Sue—"

"Like I care what her name is," Brenna interrupted.

"Well, I knew her a long time ago. But since you, Bren, there hasn't been another woman. I hadn't even been tempted. I only want you. I want to be married to you. I want us to be a family. I want our baby to grow up, knowing she has a mother and a father."

Brenna thought she would die from the ache in her chest. She wanted so much to believe Dylan, but she needed more from this man. She wouldn't settle for anything less than love. "It won't work, Dylan. We can't keep pretending everything is perfect between us."

"We didn't have any trouble getting along before," he protested.

"But you don't need me now. Your leg is almost a hundred percent. It's just gratitude you're feeling. Please, take me back to my house." She had to get away from him. She started toward the truck.

Dylan came after her. When he turned her around, she could see the desperation in his eyes. "Bren, you have to listen," he insisted, then released her and took a step back. "Damn, I'm no good at this… I want to say all the right things, but it's hard to know how to start." He raked his fingers through his hair and his shoulders slumped. "Ah, hell, here goes. You want to know why I was so desperate to get back on the circuit? It was because it was the only place I felt like I belonged. People didn't judge me as long as I stayed on the bull the full eight seconds and scored high. I gave them a show.

"But sometimes I couldn't outrun the loneliness. And sometimes it got bad, too. When our mother ignored the fact that her husband degraded and abused her sons. Wyatt handled it better than I did. He'd always known what he wanted, then went to find his family. I ran off to the rodeo. That was the only place I felt important. Then my accident happened. I thought I'd lost everything. I wanted to give up." His gaze locked with hers. "Until you walked through the door. Stubborn and bossy…and beautiful." His voice softened. "You made me realize how miserable I was." He sucked air into his lungs.

"God, Brenna, you have no idea how much I need you. I didn't know myself until I messed up. You're more important to me than my next breath. I…I can't stop thinking about you. I didn't know how wonderful it would be to lie next to you, just watch you sleep, wishing there was a way that I could tell you how I felt…but not knowing how. Afraid that you'd push me away."

Brenna stayed rooted to the spot, unable to move, aching to wrap her arms around this precious man.

His eyes searched hers. "God, Bren…I love you…so much I can't stand it." He came to her, placed his hand against her stomach. "And I love this baby. I promise you I'll do my best to be a good father." His eyes filled. "Damn, I wish I could say it right… I brought you here, to show you that I was going to put down roots. That I wasn't going to risk my life anymore."

Brenna's body grew light. "Oh, Dylan." She touched his face. "Oh, you said it perfectly. You said everything I needed to hear. I love you, too."

He smiled then. "You do?"

She nodded. "I've never felt about anyone the way I feel about you. No one—"

She was silenced when his mouth covered hers in a kiss that quickly grew intense. He tried to show her how desperate he was for her. He'd realized in the last week that she was the woman he was meant to love. When he broke off, they were both breathless. "So are you going to give us another chance?"

She giggled with excitement. "I don't know. I thought blondes were your type."

He pulled her against him. "You're the only type I want…forever."

"That's a long time. Sure you won't get bored?"

Before he could answer, he felt something against his stomach. He pulled back, looking amazed. "Was that the baby?"

She nodded. "She's been moving a lot lately."

"Oh, man, and I missed it."

"You're here now. And we'll share it all now…Daddy."

He cupped her face. "And I'm going to love her as much as her mama. And I love you a lot." He kissed her again and again. This time his hands skimmed over her stomach to her breasts. She moaned and moved against him.

"I want you, Bren," he breathed.

"I want you, too," she said. "I wish we were back at the cottage."

"I may just be able to accommodate the lady." He lifted her up in his arms.

"Dylan!" She gasped. "You shouldn't carry me."

He started up the rise toward the trailer with a grin on his face; his leg felt great. "Thanks to you, I can do a lot of things I never thought I could. The best is loving you. Did I ever thank you for making me whole again?"

"Many times," she said. "Now, stop wasting time talking, I want to see 'the devil' in action."

He grinned. "Believe me, it will be my pleasure."

Epilogue

"Hello, little darlin'," Dylan crooned at the new baby daughter in his arms.

Sarah Ann Gentry had been born just an hour ago. And with her daddy coaching her mama, she came into the world with a loud wail. She weighed a respectable seven pounds and two ounces and measured eighteen inches long. The gorgeous little girl had her mother's big brown eyes and a crown of red hair.

"She's so tiny," he whispered, then glanced at Brenna lying in the hospital bed. She looked tired, but more beautiful than he'd ever seen her.

"You wouldn't say that if you were the one who'd delivered her." Brenna smiled as she took her daughter from him. "And I'd do it all over again to get this one."

Dylan sat down on the bed. He couldn't stop looking at the miracle in her arms. He shook his head, feeling tears fill his eyes. "I've got to be the luckiest guy in the world."

"I think we both are, especially now that the house is finished. We can take our daughter to her new home."

Yes, their two-story, five-bedroom home had been completed just last week and the furniture had been arriving daily. In a few days when they'd left the hospital with Sarah, they would all truly be going home.

"And the first thing I'm going to do is to carry my bride over the threshold." He leaned forward and kissed her. "I love you so much," he said. "Even more than I thought possible."

She touched his cheek. "And to think I once had to compete with a bull."

"Never again," he told her.

In the past months since Dylan had confessed his feelings to Brenna, he'd never once regretted his decision to leave the rodeo circuit. Of course, he'd had plenty to keep him busy with building the house and opening the bull-riding school at the Rocking R. Already full, he had to turn applicants away. Best of all, he was only working a half mile away, and he could go home and see his wife and daughter anytime.

He placed another kiss on Brenna's lips. "It's sure going to be tough to stay away from you for the next six weeks."

"It's good discipline for you," she teased.

Before Dylan could argue, a knock sounded on the hospital-room door and Brenna's parents peeked in. Wyatt followed, helping his pregnant wife, Maura, who was expecting twins, a boy and a girl, in eight weeks.

"Can we see our new granddaughter?" Maggie Farren asked.

"Sure." Dylan's chest puffed out. He stepped aside so his in-laws could get a look at Sarah. All the aunts and uncles crowded around, too. If Dylan had learned anything in his six-month marriage to Brenna, it was that family was everything.

Dylan thought about his own family, his wife, daughter and his half-brothers. A year ago he had been alone. Never again.

Hank sat in the saddle and looked over Mustang Valley, as he had nearly every day of the past forty years. The serene valley hadn't changed much. The herd of wild mustangs still roamed the pasture.

But Hank wasn't alone anymore.

Since the widower had taken in three wild boys twenty-five years ago his solitude had disappeared, and he liked it that way. Now, his family had grown more than he'd ever dreamed. Three more Randell boys had come to the valley to live, expanding the family to six sons. All the brothers had married beautiful wives, giving him ten grandchildren with the recent arrival of Sarah, and Dana and Jared's baby daughter, Cassie. And two more were due to arrive soon.

"Oh, Jack, you've missed so much with your sons." Hank thought about the man who'd taken off, leaving three young boys. A man who'd selfishly used women. "Your loss was my gain. Thank you."

The sound of voices and laughter brought Hank back to the present. The older grandchildren came riding in on horseback, led by Brandon. Soon to follow were the younger ones in the horse-drawn wagon they used for the guests.

Chance, Cade and Travis were on their mounts and came up beside Hank. Chance spoke. "Jared and Wyatt are setting up the barbecue. You ready to fire it up?"

"We probably should start it before the kids get restless."

The brothers rode off to take care of the task. Hank turned to see Ella come out of the newly repaired honeymoon cabin. He climbed down and walked to her.

"Is everything ready?" he asked.

"Everything is perfect," she told him. "All the repairs are completed. We brought in food and flowers and the rest is up to the couple."

She smiled and he suddenly realized how much he'd depended on this woman over the years. Whatever would he do without her?

"It was a good idea you had, surprising Dylan and Brenna with the cabin for the weekend," he said.

"Well, their honeymoon was interrupted rather abruptly by that tornado. And after six weeks of parenthood, it's a great time for a couple to rediscover each other."

"You're such a romantic," he teased.

She made a snorting sound. "So, after all these years you finally noticed."

"I notice a lot of things." His gaze met hers. "Especially when they pertain to you."

He watched as emotion clouded her eyes. "Why, Hank Barrett, don't you go getting all mushy on me. I wouldn't know how to handle it."

He surprised himself, and her, when he pulled Ella into his arms and kissed her gently on her shocked mouth. "I just needed to tell you that I care about you. The boys think of you as a mother. And all the grandkids call you Grandma. I'd call you one special woman, Ella. Thank you for coming into my life."

She relaxed in his arms momentarily, then pulled back. "It was my pleasure." Ella's eyes watered, but there was a smile on her face. And Hank realized that smile had been something he'd been looking forward to for years.

"No, it's been mine." He took her hand and together they turned and watched the children running up and down the rise. The adults were busy spreading out the blankets, arranging things for the picnic. The brothers were talking and joking with each other. They weren't just family, they were also friends.

"You know, Hank, we are awfully lucky to have all this."

"I know," he began, not wanting to let go of Ella's hand. He wanted to share this moment with her. "I was just sending up a thanks to good old Jack Randell for letting me raise his boys. I wouldn't even mind if there were more of his kids out there."

She groaned. "Well, if that happens, I hope it's a girl who comes to Mustang Valley."

Hank didn't care. He'd been blessed with so much. He had it all. All he could ever want or need was right here in Mustang Valley. His family.

*   *   *   *   *

In Camelot's Shadow

An Arthurian tale comes to life....

From the wilds of Moreland to the court of Camelot, a woman searches for her true powers....

Risa of the Morelands refuses to be a sacrifice. Promised to the evil Euberacon, the infamous sorcerer, Risa flees armed only with her strong will and bow. When Risa stumbles upon Sir Gawain returning to Camelot, she believes she has discovered the perfect refuge: Camelot, noble Arthur's court. The sorcerer would never dare to come after her while she was under the protection of the Knights of the Round Table! Clearly, Risa has underestimated Euberacon's desire to have her as his wife.

On sale February 24. Visit your local bookseller.

SILHOUETTE *Romance* ®

presents

DADDY'S LITTLE MEMENTO
by Teresa Carpenter
(Silhouette Romance #1716)

**When Samantha Dell showed up
on Alex Sullivan's doorstep with
his chubby-cheeked baby in tow, she
never imagined Alex would want to
be a full-time parent—or her husband!**

Available April 2004 at your favorite retail outlet.

SILHOUETTE *Romance*®

COMING NEXT MONTH

#1714 THE PIED PIPER'S BRIDE—Myrna Mackenzie
The Brides of Red Rose
The women of Red Rose needed men—and they'd decided sexy Chicago bigwig Parker Monroe was going to help find them! But Parker wasn't interested in populating his hometown with eligible bachelors. Enter their secret weapon, Parker's former neighbor. But how was the love-shy Ellie Donahue supposed to entice her former crush to save the town without sacrificing her heart a second time?

#1715 THE LAST CRAWFORD BACHELOR—
Judy Christenberry
From the Circle K
Assistant District Attorney Michael Crawford was perfectly happy being the last unmarried Crawford son and he didn't need Daniele Langston messing it up. But when Dani aroused his protective instincts, his fetching co-*worker* became his co-*habitant*. Now this business-minded bachelor was thinking less about the courtroom and more about the bedroom....

#1716 DADDY'S LITTLE MEMENTO—Teresa Carpenter
The only convenient thing about Samantha Dell's marriage was her becoming a stepmother to precious eleven-month-old nephew Gabe. Living with Gabe's seductive reluctant daddy didn't work into her lifelong plans. *And getting pregnant by him?* Well, that certainly wasn't part of the arrangement! Would falling in love with her heartthrob husband be next?

#1717 BAREFOOT AND PREGNANT—Colleen Faulkner
Career-driven Ellie Montgomery had everything a girl could want—except a husband! But *The Husband Finder* was going to change that. Except, according to the book, her perfect match, former bad-boy Zane Keaton, was definitely Mr. Wrong! But a few of Zane's knee-weakening, heart-stopping kisses had Ellie wondering if he might be marriage material after all.

SRCNM0304